WHATEVER IT TAKES

CARDINAL SINS: LUST

BROOKLYN BAILEY

This is a work of fiction. Names, characters, businesses, places, events, and incidents are either the products of the author's imagination or used in a fictitious manner. Any resemblance to actual persons, living or dead, or actual events is purely coincidental.

Any trademarks, service marks, product names, or named features are assumed to be the property of their respective owners and are used only for reference. There is no implied endorsement.

Whatever It Takes, Cardinal Sins: Lust
Copyright © 2022 Brooklyn Bailey
All rights reserved.

Cover Design by Germancreativ on Fiverr

eBook ISBN: 978-1-959199-12-0
Paperback ISBN: 978-1-959199-08-3

❧ Created with Vellum

ENHANCE YOUR READING

To Enhance Your Reading of Whatever It Takes read the Trivia Page near the end of the book prior to opening chapter #1.

No Spoilers-I promise.

DEDICATION

To my best friend, Dawn. For over 25 years you know the exact moment I need to see your face or hear your voice. You never judge my unkept hair, lack of makeup, or my wearing the same t-shirt for multiple days. You take me as I am and love me for it. You are the greatest therapist and I'm forever thankful.

PROLOGUE

Lewis

Twenty hours of travel wear on me. I long to check into the hotel, take a shower, and catch a nap. But I can't. I need to be with my family. Carter's death won't be real until I'm with his family—my family. Ryan. I need to be with Ryan. Her pain trumps mine.

I park my rental car at the curb, noting there are no visiting cars in the driveway. *Odd.* Ryan and Ian should be surrounded by family, work colleagues, neighbors, and friends.

I peel myself from the driver's seat, suck in a deep breath, and head for the front door. I raise my knuckles to knock as the front door slowly opens, revealing Ryan holding a sleeping Ian in her arms.

"Shh," she urges, motioning for me to enter. "He's teething and not sleeping much. I have to preserve it when I can."

I nod, at a loss for words. Before me stands my best friend since college, my sister-in-law, cradling my nephew in her arms. She's thin and pale with dark circles under her eyes. Twenty-four hours ago, my identical twin, her husband, died in a freak construction site accident. She's alone in this tiny house with a baby; life's not fair. This strong, brilliant woman now stands before me, exhausted and broken.

Near the sofa, I extend my arms. "Let me hold him," I offer.

"He's the only thing anchoring me; if I'm not holding him, I might not be able to keep it together." She forces a tiny twitch of her mouth that I'm sure she means to be a smile.

"What can I do to help?" I ask, keeping my voice low, not wanting to wake Ian.

She shakes her head, eyes closed.

"The funeral home promised to call me this afternoon," she whispers, looking down to her son. "The hospital already released his… body." She lifts her eyes to mine, still slowly walking the perimeter of the room. "I don't know what to do. It will be a small funeral." Still whispering, she shakes her head. "I fear it will only be the two of us."

My eyes squint as I mull over her words. *"Small funeral of just the two of us."* Dad's gone, and Mom's in the Alzheimer unit in Florida. I have no other siblings and no extended family. *Ryan only had our family, but what about the neighbors, fellow workers, and friends?*

"Ryan," I say, forgetting to lower my voice. I wince. Continuing, I whisper, "Have the neighbors stopped by or his work friends?"

Head sagging, she shakes it from side to side.

I close the distance between us, carefully pulling her into a hug.

"We only moved in a couple of months ago," she sobs quietly. "When Carter had to take off weeks to settle your mom into the nursing home, he pissed off the guys at work…"

Ian stirs in her arms at the sound of her crying. This time, I don't ask. I maneuver him into my arms.

"Many of my colleagues work at home like I do…" She shrugs as if it's no big deal.

She's alone, utterly alone, and I work on the other side of the world.

"May I make the arrangements for you?" I offer, struggling for a way to help her.

She nods. "I'll get you a copy of his wishes we put on paper when we had Ian."

I shake my head. "That's not necessary; I have my own copy."

"How rude of me," she murmurs. "You've been traveling forever. Would you like a drink?"

"I'll fix it," I state, lightly brushing Ian's little forehead. "Can I get one for you, too?"

She nods.

"Ian's content and quiet. If there's something you need to do, go ahead," I urge, knowing she needs a shower, a nap, or even to soak in a warm bath.

"I'll only be a minute," she states, stepping into her bedroom.

"We men have this, don't we?" I whisper to my tiny, still sleeping nephew. "We can fix Mommy a drink and give her some alone time. Yes, we can," I coo.

I hate that he's three months old, and this is the first time I've visited him. An uncle's first visit shouldn't be at a child's father's funeral. *I've really messed things up; it's time I remedy that.*

When I took this three-year contract in Dubai to escape the woman I love and can't be with, I didn't take into account the life-altering events that might occur in my absence. After returning from my twin's funeral, I plan to work myself to the bone for months, so I can return home sooner rather than later. In my first year away, my mother was admitted to an Alzheimer long-term care facility, Carter and Ryan had Ian, and then Carter died. In my attempt to escape a romance, I left my family vulnerable.

My new plan involves me completing my three-year contract a year early. If possible, I'd back out now and move back to the States, but I must see the transition through to completion. Until I return, I'll be diligent in my email communication and phone calls to Ryan. The time difference delayed me often in the past. Now, I vow to reply within a day. She's alone, raising a baby, and I need to support her in the only way I can. We've scheduled our twice weekly video calls. With the nine-hour time difference, she'll call me at ten, before bed, and I'll answer at seven, before my workday begins.

Having never been a parent or married, my words of support may not be helpful, but at least I can listen and offer opinions.

I promised Carter at his graveside that I would take care of Ryan and Ian, and I plan to keep that promise by every means possible.

Three Months Later

As I walk home as quickly as my legs will allow, I internally curse the one meeting I had to attend before I could call Ryan as she requested in her frantic email. It must be important if she asked me to call, regardless of the time difference. I could have taken it at the office, but I thought it best to dial from the privacy of my apartment.

I barely latch the door behind me as my thumbs find her contact and tap to connect. I hold my breath as the call rings once then twice before she answers. I do not hear her greeting; my eyes take in the frazzled woman on the screen.

Ryan's crying, actively crying, and my heart breaks. Her eyes are swollen, red, and tired, her cheeks blotchy and wet. I force myself to snap to attention, listening to her words.

"He's worse… It's…" She sobs loudly then looks over her shoulder.

My eyes follow to see Ian in a hospital bed, too many tubes, wires, and machines hooked up to him. My heart plummets, and my stomach roils.

"Ryan, honey…" I attempt to calm her in order to find out what's wrong with Ian. "Take a few deep breaths then talk to me."

I can hear her breathing as my eyes remain glued to my nephew. He's so little and pale.

"It's leukemia," Ryan states between sobs. "Lewis, my baby has leukemia…"

Concrete. From my chest down, my body feels heavy and cold like concrete. *This is the year from hell.* Ryan's world crumbles piece by piece, and I, her best friend, hide halfway around the world, locked into a contract I must see to completion.

Leukemia. What do I know of leukemia? It's a cancer, a cancer of the blood, I think. I believe I've heard of people in remission; maybe there's hope.

"Lewis, can you hear me?" Ryan asks, her face too close to the camera of her cell phone.

"Yes. Sorry," I respond, not wanting to add to her panic.

"They've admitted him. We're at Blank's Children's Hospital," she shares. "It wasn't teething; I thought he was teething…"

"Ry," I butt in. "There was no way for you to know. The symptoms were similar to teething."

"Until they weren't," she argues. "When his fever didn't come down, when he had bruises… I should have…"

"Stop!" I yell, immediately regretting it. "You'll drive yourself crazy with all of the 'should haves'. You took him to the pediatrician, and now he's getting treatment." I fight the anger and tears that grow within me. "You are *not* to blame."

She nods, wiping away her tears.

"What do you need? What can I do?" I ask, feeling as if my hands are tied behind my back since I'm so far away.

"Just…" She pulls in a short, shaky breath. "Just be here for me."

"You know I am," I state, feeling helpless. "Calls and emails anytime, day or night."

She nods.

"Is he…" I swallow the large clog in my throat. "Is he in pain?"

Ryan shakes her head. "He's sedated and very sleepy. They have him on a ventilator; he's not breathing on his own." Again, she breaks into body-trembling sobs.

I need to be in Des Moines. I promised Carter I would be. She needs somebody. I should be there so she's not alone.

"Ryan, honey." I break into her crying. "Take a seat, grab a box of tissues, and tell me everything."

1

LEWIS

Six Months Later

Nervously, I extend my photo ID to the desk clerk to prove my relation to Ian. The staff member taps several keys on his computer, pauses for a moment, then hands me a sticker name badge to wear. It identifies me as a visitor and gives my full name. I follow his directions, stepping through the door when I hear the buzzer sound to unlock it.

Although he gave me specific directions, I didn't listen. My nerves over seeing my nephew play havoc on my mind. Now, I must read all signs and follow the arrows. I pass through the hallways, ride the elevator, and finally complete the maze, entering the pediatric oncology center. I introduce myself at the nurses' station where, thanks to my name badge, they tuck my two small, rolling suitcases into a nearby closet, and I'm escorted to Ian's room while I'm instructed to adhere to all posted protocols.

My mind doesn't have time to process the meaning of 'posted protocols.' The sight of Ian in his hospital bed is a punch in the gut. I enter the room. Ryan naps, upright in the hospital chair at his bedside. Ian sleeps, again tangled in too many tubes. I pause inside the large doorway. My little man lies before me, so weak, so little, so lifeless.

I press my palm to the plastic curtain surrounding his bed, imagining I'm holding his hand. "I'm here," I murmur. "Uncle Lewis is here."

"Lewis?" Ryan rasps sleepily.

"Hey," I greet, turning to face her.

She looks as exhausted as I feel after my 21-hour flight. I know that her exhaustion is bone deep, and mine will fade tomorrow. I waited too long to return. I should have broken my contract the minute Carter died. If not then, when Ian was diagnosed. *My family is more important than any job or money.*

"What are..." She clears her dry throat, tears welling in her eyes. "Why didn't you tell me you were coming?"

I motion for her to stay when she attempts to join me. I step to her, kneeling in front of her as she remains seated.

"It was a last-minute thing," I lie, placing my hands on her jean-covered knees. "Surprise," my voice lacks enthusiasm.

Tears spill from her tired eyes, and her hand flies to cover her mouth.

"Hey, now," I soothe. "Don't cry. You know I hate it when you cry."

I pull her chest to mine, arms securing her in place. I hold her for several moments, allowing her to release her pent-up emotions. Leaning back, leaving my hands upon her shoulders, I look her in the eyes.

She shakes her head, wiping her tears. "He may be discharged tomorrow," she shares.

"Good. I can't wait to hold him and spoil him rotten." I attempt to lighten the mood.

"How long..." She takes a long breath in. "How long..."

"I finished my contract," I state. "I'm back in the States for good."

A wide smile shines back at me. I put it there, and I plan to make it my daily goal to help her smile despite all that is going on in her life.

"When will you need to be in Kansas City?" she asks hesitantly.

I shake my head. "As of yesterday, I'm..." I struggle for words. I'm not retired, but I'm kind of unemployed. "I'm looking for a new job."

I watch as shock, confusion, then relief flip through her eyes.

"I promised Carter I'd be around to help the two of you," I share. "I plan to keep my promise."

She's unable to speak and simply nods in understanding.

"Can I stay with you?" I ask my sister-in-law, already knowing her response. "I don't want to add to your stress. I want to be close to help you care for Ian, though."

She nods, smiling. "It will be like we're back in college." She chuckles hollowly.

The woman before me resembles the girl I befriended in my junior year of college. Her tired eyes display dark circles below them, and her disheveled hair and wrinkled clothes are a billboard to her current predicament.

Ian's been in the hospital for five days, and it looks as if she's never left his bedside. I don't blame her. I just flew 21 hours then drove straight to the hospital. It's apparent she needs a break, but now's not the time to suggest it.

"Do you sleep in that chair?" I ask, pointing to the turquoise, hardback one beside Ian's bed.

She points to the far corner of the room. "The nurses found me a cot to sleep on."

I nod, noting it can't be much more comfortable than the chair.

"Any changes today?" I ask, attempting to fill the silence.

"His counts have risen steadily, the antibiotics are working, and he's breathing much better," she shares, a frail smile upon her gaunt face.

"Well, that's great news."

"On his evening rounds, the doctor said he may be discharged in the morning."

I close the distance between us, wrapping my arms around her, squeezing tightly. *He's going home. He's not cured, but going home is good. I'm in over my head here, but even I know leaving the hospital is a good sign.*

2

LEWIS

That Night

The house is too small and eerily quiet. I'm exhausted from my travel time from Dubai to Iowa, yet I lay here, staring at the ceiling of the guest room in the house my deceased brother shared with his wife.

I've been back in the United States not even a day, and I can't get the woman I love off my mind. I took the contract in Dubai to move as far away from her as I could to prevent me from acting on my feelings for her. Years later, I'm barely back on the same continent as her, and I can't sleep. Every time I shut my eyes, she's there.

After hours in bed, now I imagine her even as my eyes stare at the ceiling. I've attempted to think of her as forbidden fruit, a married woman, but that doesn't ease my need for her. I've battled with doing the right thing for over three years now. Before I left, I spent more than a year sleeping with woman after woman, one-night stand after one-night stand, and still, she haunts me. I can't run away, and I can't get her out of my system; my mind, my body, and my heart continue to gravitate toward her.

Too tired to fight another minute, I close my eyes, allowing the fantasy to engulf me.

It never fails that I wake up uncomfortable after I dream of her. I ease from the bed, heading to the shower in the only bathroom in this little house. As I'm alone, I forego the cold shower, opting for hot. I waste no time to remedy my uncomfortable situation. I don't even have to close my eyes; I imagine she's in the shower with me.

"Y-E-S!" My growl reverberates off the tiled walls.

I take my time, my eyes closed as my breath settles. Then, my eyes fly open. I'm suddenly very aware what I have done in Ryan's shower. I search the space, only finding her vanilla body wash. I'll need to run to the store in the morning. Not wanting to smell like food, I use her shampoo to wash my hair then rinse off the rest of my body. I scan the space, ensuring no evidence remains before turning off the water, drying myself, and falling back into bed.

3
RYAN

The Next Day

Lewis drives Ian and me home from the hospital a bit before noon. He kept his promise to help, bringing Ian's car seat with him upon his return.

"I picked up the house, bought some groceries, and finished the laundry," he mentions, as if these are common daily tasks for him.

I can't help the smile that slips upon my face at the thought of Lewis in his tailored suit, up to his elbows in dishes and laundry.

"What?" he asks, glancing at me then back to the road in front of us.

I shrug, shaking my head. "In college, did you ever dream you'd be working in Dubai, and I'd be working from home?"

"My life couldn't be farther from what I dreamt," he replies immediately.

"Would you change anything?" I ask. "I mean, anything in your ability to be changed."

I know my answer. Since I can't change Carter's accident or Ian's illness, the only thing I might want to change would be us moving to Des Moines. We could have stayed in Florida with his parents or moved to Kansas City when Lewis did. Rousing from my thoughts, I look at him.

Lewis

Ryan's question hits home. Rarely a day goes by that I don't wish I had the woman I love in my arms—in my bed. I waited and missed my chance; now, I'm alone, and she has a family. I regret my hesitation every day. I don't share this with Ryan. I don't need to. She knows I have "lady troubles." I bet her niggling to get more details will intensify with me back in the States now. She's like a dog with a bone.

"You'll let me know if there's anything else I can do to help, right?" I do my best to deter her attention. I chance a glance, only to find her eyes squinting, assessing. *Yep. She's going to keep digging for information.*

I attempt to keep my attention on driving but can't hide the smirk growing on my face. I've missed my best friend, even the nosy, prying parts of her.

―――

"I'm not sure what I have for dinner tonight," Ryan states, forehead against the passenger window, staring blankly at the passing scenery.

"I grabbed everything I need to cook for you tonight," I brag, glancing at her then quickly back on the road.

"What will it be: ramen, frozen pizza, or canned soup?" Ryan asks.

I feel her gaze upon the side of my face. "Your memory must be slipping in your old age," I tease. "You were the Ramen and soup queen. I fixed new recipes all the time for us."

Her smile grows infinitesimally, and my pride inflates. It's already working; I'm helping her to find a reason to smile.

"I'm making pasta with garlic bread," I brag. "I plan to feed you then tuck you into bed for some much-needed rest."

"With jet lag, you need rest, too," she attempts to argue.

"I slept like the dead last night." I flinch as soon as the words leave my lips and scramble to move past the inappropriate comment. "I'm sure I'll sleep well tonight and be at 100 percent by the morning."

I glance at her while stopped at a red light. "Ry, I can't have you getting worn down or sick."

She bites her lips and looks away without arguing.

4

LEWIS

At Home

Ryan holds open the door as I carry Ian, sleeping on my shoulder, into the house. Without direction, I place him in his baby bed then join Ryan in the kitchen.

Bent over the kitchen island, her forehead between her hands, I approach cautiously, trying to ascertain if she's crying or simply exhausted. She doesn't look up to acknowledge my presence.

"I feel safer with him here," she states, head still in hands. "I'm on high alert the entire hospital stay, the oppressive truth of his health like a dark, heavy cloud over me. At home, I tell myself he's healthier or the doctors wouldn't have released him. At home, I still have hope we'll make it through."

I place my hands on hers as she now stands across the island from me. We stare for several long moments, our unspoken thoughts understood by the other.

"Okay." I break the long silence. "Off with you," I order, pointing away from the kitchen. "You relax while I make dinner."

"If I sit down, I may not be able to get back up," she confesses honestly.

Pulling pans from the cabinet beneath the island, I instruct, "Then, get everything ready that Ian might need for the night, and get your stuff ready for bed. After that, you can come keep me company while I perform art over the stovetop." I try to add a bit of levity to lighten the mood.

Upon her exit, I focus on seasoning my red sauce, boiling the pasta, and warming the garlic bread to perfection. It's my hope that the heavy carbs meal will make Ryan quickly find deep sleep.

"I can't eat another bite," Ryan announces, pushing her half-eaten plate away. "I haven't had a meal like that since…"

We're silent, both knowing the words to complete her statement are "since Carter died." His memory lingers in every room of this tiny home he created with her. Hell, one need only look to Ian to see the miniature version of my brother. For the last year, the constant reminders had to weigh heavily on Ryan. It's wrong that I'm grateful for my time overseas without memories of my twin everywhere I looked. My absence allowed me to grieve; I fear her living here with Ian and his illness prevented Ryan from working through her own grief.

"So, will you be looking for a job in K.C. or…?" Ryan asks.

I wonder how long she's been wanting to ask me that question.

"I'd like to stay in Des Moines," I answer honestly. "If you'll have me, I'd like to live with the two of you. And as far as work goes, I think I'm going to take time off and write the book Carter and I started in high school."

Ryan's stunned expression is freaking adorable. I reach across the table, place my index finger under her chin, and close her open mouth. She bites her lips, eyes blinking fast in an attempt to keep unshed tears from falling.

"I still have the notebooks the two of you wrote in," she states. "They are in the guest room closet in a box labeled 'high school.'"

"Are you serious?" I ask. "I can't believe you kept them."

"Well, Carter's the one that kept them," she confesses. "I haven't had time or energy to go through…"

The lights on the baby monitor blink, and sounds of Ian whining emit from its speaker. I motion for Ryan to remain seated, hopping up and moving quickly down the hall.

"Here she is," I murmur softly. "Here's Mommy." I slide him from my chest into her lap at the island.

While she fusses over him, I start a warm bath for her, complete with bubbles from her body wash, before returning to the kitchen. Ryan sways back and forth, comforting her son in her arms as I tuck leftovers into the refrigerator and load the dishwasher.

"My turn," I announce, arms open toward them. "We'll have male-bonding time while you slip into the warm tub."

She opens her mouth to argue, but I continue, "If you don't hurry, there will be water and bubbles all over the bathroom floor."

This lights a fire in her.

"Bye-bye, Mommy," I say and assist Ian in waving. "Now," I turn him in my arms to face me. "Little man, what will it be? Should we watch ESPN or Animal Planet?"

Of course, Ian remains silent in my arms as I move us into the recliner.

"This is a man's chair." I educate my nephew. "This is where we'll watch football games, baseball games, and movies."

Ian's tiny blue eyes take me in. I wonder what he's thinking. *Could it be, 'Who is this stranger?' Or is he confused by my resemblance to his father?* I know infants recognize their parents, but as they grow, do they remember them? Can memories fade during an absence of several months? I don't want to confuse him; I'm his uncle, and that's different from his father.

5

RYAN

Later

I must admit, soaking in the bath Lewis filled feels divine. For over twenty minutes, I allow my muscles to relax in the warm bubbles. I quirk my head to one side then crane my neck closer to the bathroom door. *Nothing.* In my small house, I should hear Ian's whimpers and Lewis talking to him. *Nothing. Not even the television.*

Inspecting my hands, I find my fingertips pruny; it's time I emerge. I wrap my terry cloth robe over my arms and secure it tightly around my waist. I quickly dry myself then slowly open the bathroom door, hoping to hear where the guys are.

I tiptoe down the hall, peeking into Ian's room to find it empty. At the living room doorway, I see the TV frozen on the menu screen and Lewis asleep. His long body extends the length of the recliner, and Ian sleeps soundly upon his chest, his little thumb in his mouth.

I quickly and quietly fetch my cell phone and snap a photo. I must record this moment: Uncle Lewis asleep, one hand on Ian's back—securing him to his chest—the other holding the TV remote control.

Lewis

"I'm the luckiest man on Earth," I murmur, my mouth less than an inch from hers.

"Lewis, please," she begs, her chest arching toward mine.

My eyes pop wide open, taking in the dark guest room and my empty bed. Damn my subconscious. He's my worst enemy. My interludes in slumber are the cruelest form of torture. They only fuel my longing for my forbidden love.

I untwist the sheet from my legs, angrily rising from the bed. I stomp to the door. I need to put distance between me and the bed, me and the fantasies of what might have been. I intend to make my way to the kitchen in search of water but halt when I find Ryan in the hallway. In two long strides, I stand near where she sits on the floor outside Ian's door, her knees tight to her chest.

"Hey," I quietly greet, sliding down the wall across from her. "Is he...Ian...?"

She shakes her head, a small smile upon her face. "He's sleeping. I just needed to be closer to him."

"Can't sleep, huh?" I ask, hoping my hands conceal the uncomfortable situation I have.

I don't want to give Ryan the wrong idea or give her reason to kick me out of her house. I'm here to help make her life easier and support her.

Ryan adjusts her legs into a yoga pose before answering, "It's hard to sleep. I have too many scenarios playing in my mind. The farther I am from Ian, the more panicked I am." She shrugs. "It's hard to think positive..." Her statement hangs heavy in the night.

I search for appropriate words. I don't want to belittle her fears; she's been alone on the front lines with Ian. As much as I want to encourage her to remain positive, now is not the time.

"How often do you spend the night outside his door?" I ask.

"Sometimes, I sleep on the floor next to his crib. I've slept out here, too. I want to bring him into my bed, but I've read that's a hard habit to break. I can't sleep next to him in the hospital, so I don't do it here," she explains.

"Would you like me to move his crib into your bedroom tomorrow?" I offer.

Her head tilts to the side in thought. I won't be able to solve every issue, but this seems one I can make easier for her.

"Maybe," she hedges. "Let me think about it."

I nod, hoping she can see the movement in the shadows.

"Why don't you go back to bed?" I suggest. "I have my days and nights mixed up, so I can keep an eye on him for you tonight."

"That's not necessary. I have a baby monitor," she replies. "Sometimes, I need to see him."

"Tomorrow, I'll go buy a baby monitor with video feed," I offer. "You'll be able to stay in your comfy bed and watch him at the same time."

"I'm so glad you're back," she states.

Lewis

A few nights later, unable to sleep, I fetch water from the kitchen. I swing by Ian's room before returning to mine. He sleeps like an angel. I shake my head. This tiny human endures more than any kid should. I say a prayer to keep Ian safe until I can put my plan into action.

What's that? I tilt my head toward the door. It's Ryan. Slowly, I creep to her bedroom door, peeking through the crack, I see she's lying on her bed, her back to the door. I watch as the shadow of her body shakes with her muted sobs. My hand reaches for the knob but stops when I hear her whisper through her tears. She's trying to keep quiet; she doesn't want Ian or me to see her cry. In the quiet darkness, alone in her room, this strong woman lets down her guard.

Every part of me longs to climb in bed behind her, wrap my arms around her, and comfort her as she attempts to release her pain. She wouldn't allow it; she wants to always appear strong. I've got to step up more. I need to lift her burden.

"I'll make this better," I silently vow. I back down the hallway without making a sound, prepared to tiptoe to my room, but opt to remain in Ian's room. I place my hand on his back; it slowly rises and falls in time with his breaths. Each breath Ian takes is a testament to his fighting spirit. There are two types of pain: the pain that hurts and the pain that changes you forever.

"Hang on, little man. Hang on. Help is on its way."

The next night, with Ian resting peacefully in his crib, I return to the living room to find Ryan missing. *I wonder where she went.* I check the kitchen and then her bedroom. I turn toward the hallway, pausing when I hear a sob from the bathroom.

Damn! She's crying again. I'd give anything to keep her tears from forming. *I'm trying. Why does my plan need to take a year instead of days or weeks?* I'm thankful I'm working on a plan, but I wish we had more than one option in the works. My feet feel like concrete blocks as I step toward the door separating her from me. I lift my fist to knock, pausing for a moment. I shake my head. I must do this, so I knock twice.

"Ryan, honey?" I call, my head leaning against the door between us.

"Just a minute," she calls.

"Ry, I'm coming in," I warn as I turn the knob.

"Lewis!" she warns.

I stand stunned, frozen in place. I expected a crying Ryan on the floor. Instead, I find her curled up into a ball in the empty bathtub. The sound of her sobs echo in the surrounding porcelain. I take a seat on the closed toilet lid, reaching for her.

"Come here, honey," I urge, taking her hand in mine, slowly pulling her toward me.

Her lower lip protrudes as if pouting as she attempts to stifle her sobs.

"C'mon." I pat my lap, and she climbs in.

I wrap my arms tightly around her torso, urging her head to lay on my shoulder.

"It's okay," I soothe. "I'm here; you're no longer alone."

I squeeze her close to me, wishing I could absorb all her pain and fears. In researching online, I learned that sometimes she doesn't need words. She just needs to know I'm here for her, I'll do anything for her, and she's no longer alone on Ian's journey.

It won't be easy, but I'm putting my career and desire on hold to support my best friend and my nephew.

6

RYAN

Later That Week

Unable to sleep for the third night this week, I sit with my elbow propping my head up as I enjoy a late-night bowl of cereal. Lost in my thoughts, I don't hear the approaching footsteps or the creaking floorboards.

"Still not able to sleep?" Lewis greets, plopping onto the stool beside mine before stealing my spoon and helping himself to a bite of my cereal.

"It's just like college," I mention in reference to our many late-night snacks where he ate my food instead of making his own.

"It still tastes better than what I would make," he teases, gently bumping his shoulder against mine.

"Why can't you sleep?" I ask between bites.

He shrugs then takes another bite.

"I bet I know why you can't sleep," I offer, pulling a notepad and pen across the island.

"Here we go," he mumbles. "Tell me, Doctor Ryan. Why can't I sleep, and why do you need that notepad?"

"I'm glad you asked," I croon. "I'm going to make a list. Now, tell me what she's like."

"Who?" Lewis plays dumb.

"Your mystery woman. The woman that led you to move halfway around the world." I smile, tapping my pen on the pad. "What's your type?"

"I've already told you," he bites.

"No," I draw out. "You've only told me she's not single. Let's make a list of attributes you look for in a woman."

Lewis shakes his head.

"You can't sleep," I remind him. "It's loneliness or thoughts of her that are haunting you. One of us should be getting laid—so spill."

His eyes widen, and his mouth opens before he squints. He does not speak.

"Hair color?" I prompt. When he shakes his head, I repeat, "Hair color?"

"Brunette," he mumbles, not at all happy with my line of questioning.

"Build? Body type?" I continue.

He squeezes his lips tightly between his teeth for several moments. Just when I think he'll refuse to humor me, he replies. "Athletic."

"Hobbies? Interests?" I ask.

"She likes sporting events live and on TV," he states. "She cusses, she talks to herself, and she prefers wine to beer…"

I quickly take notes as he describes his mystery woman. "Funny, organized, loves to plan, everybody likes her, she's at home when she's hanging with a group of guys, smart, caring…" I attempt to hide my shock that he's sharing these details.

I look up when he stops. He's smirking. That causes me to read over my notes, worried that he's not being honest. Each of these attributes describes a woman I can see Lewis with. She definitely needs to be educated, goal-oriented, and funny. I tap my pen at the bottom of the list while I contemplate the reason for his smirk.

"Happy?" he inquires, smirk still present.

I nod. "It's a starting point. I'm contemplating where to go from here…"

"Um, nowhere," he protests.

I purse my lips. "Need I remind you the goal is for you to get laid? So…"

His smirk turns into his sexy smile that I know makes all the women swoon. I raise my brow, and he taps my forehead.

"I know how your brain works," he states. "We will not be using an app or online dating. I'm not taking you as my wing-woman to pick up chicks at the grocery store, Target, or even Home Depot. You have your list; you got what you wanted. I've described her inside and out. This topic is officially closed."

I don't think so. If Lewis plans to live with us for the long-term, I need to make sure he's happy. If not, he'll eventually find a new adventure and say his goodbyes. I have a blueprint. Now, I'll be hyper alert. Surely, I can find a woman in the Des Moines area that meets all his criteria.

7

RYAN

The Next Morning

"So, tell me about your job so I can create an office workspace that's best for you," Lewis prompts.

Really? I can work sitting on the sofa if I want to, so an office is a perk. "I work online," I explain. "I receive requests via email. I create graphics, post on social media, send out author newsletters, edit manuscripts, that type of thing."

I search his face for a reaction. Nothing. Not positive. Not negative. *Hmm.*

"So," he begins, "you work heavily on the internet. How much desk space do you need? And how often do you print?"

So many questions. When he offered to create an office for us, I thought he'd throw a desk and a file cabinet above the garage. Maybe hook up some WiFi. Something easy peasy.

"I guess I need enough desk space to open a notebook." I shrug, not knowing how he will react. "I print occasionally, but 90 percent of my work is digital."

He nods.

"I mean, I'm happy on the sofa."

"Well, I will not be happy with you on the sofa," he states. "You deserve an office. You'll be much more productive in a designated workspace."

I shake my head to clear it. He's right. Two years ago, I couldn't work without my office desk.

"I blame your brother," I defend. "I think he rubbed off on me."

Lewis shakes his head with a small smile and eyes locked on me. "Your world turned upside down, and you adapted. It's human nature. No one is to blame."

That's not what I meant. I blame Carter's laissez-faire attitude for breaking me of some of my OCD and uptight ways. I fight the burning in my sinuses. I will *not* cry.

"I'm here to help, so you will work in an office." His smile reaches up to his eyes. "You'll still work from home with flexible hours; you'll just work in the office now so you can concentrate, create, and work efficiently while I'm with Ian."

Twenty-four hours later, I stand in the former apartment above the garage. It's no longer an apartment to rent; it's an office. There is room for two desktops and printer stands on the white Formica counters sitting on several two-drawer metal file cabinets, painted white to match. The counters flank three walls. Set along the fourth wall is a play area for Ian. I walk toward it for a better look.

Hand upon the white, plastic baby gate, Lewis explains, "I opted for the fencing in lieu of a playpen. It will give Ian more room for his toys and to safely roam."

I look from the area toward Lewis, proudly standing at my side.

"The mattress on the floor serves as a nap area and a soft play area," he shares.

"It's…" I clear the lump in my throat. "It's perfect. The office is perfect. Ian's area is perfect."

"I figure the small kitchenette and restroom will allow us to work longer in this area without running down the stairs into the house," he continues.

"Lewis, it's perfect," I say again. "I thought of one desk and a filing cabinet that the two of us would share. This is so much better than I'd envisioned."

His smile widens. He should be proud. He did well.

"I'll be able to focus on work and complete projects in less time without distractions." I think out loud.

"That's the plan." He chuckles.

"You're awesome!"

"Tell me something I don't know," he teases, bumping his elbow against my shoulder. "While you work here, I'll show Ian how awesome his uncle really is."

I like Lewis spending time with Ian; he'll need a man in his life.

8

RYAN

Days Later

Lewis unloads the dishwasher as I approach from the front room. With only the overhead light of the sink, from this viewpoint, he looks like his brother. Memories of Carter and me cooking and washing dishes together in this kitchen flood my mind. Carter called it our "dish dance" as we moved like a team in the tiny space.

"Ryan." Lewis's firm tone beckons me from my memories.

His tilted head and concerned eyes lead me to believe he knows I lost myself in the past. I force a slight smile, placing my glass in the sink.

"You, okay?" he asks, his large hand rubbing my back between my shoulders.

"Yep," I reply, not wanting to talk about it.

"I have an idea for a treatment to help Ian, and I think we should do it," he bluntly shares. His hand rests on my shoulder as I face him.

My brows arch in question. This seems out of left field, but as my thoughts are always on Ian's health, it's only right that his are, too.

"I'm sorry. I'm not wording this right," he apologizes, motioning for me to take a seat. "When no family member was a match for Ian, I researched other treatments in my spare time."

Spare time? He rushed to finish his contract months early to get back to us. When did he have spare time?

"Since we haven't found a bone marrow donor to match him," he explains, shaking his head, "I believe we should look into a savior sibling. A brother or sister is the best donor. We should just do it."

His words shock me. In the many days I've spent at appointments, treatments, and Ian's side in the hospital, I've heard of savior siblings. One parent I met has successfully done this. They also said they knew another family that had. I love Lewis's desire to help by any means available. However, this is not an option for me; with Carter gone, it's not an option for Ian. I don't have time to react before he continues.

"I want you to use my sperm," Lewis offers.

"You're serious?" I cough, struggling to pull in a breath.

Nodding, he states, "Let's do it."

Do it? He can't be serious. What kind of pick-up line is that? My eyes search his. *He's crazy. This idea is crazy. We can't; it wouldn't be right.*

Lewis's hands on my shoulders squeeze before he explains, "I'm Carter's identical twin. I'm the best chance to match a sibling for Ian."

Weird! No way! I shake my head and retreat.

"Stop!" Lewis gently commands, moving between me and the doorway. "I meant that we should use in vitro…" He pauses a minute, letting his words sink in before explaining. "I wasn't here. You were a pillar, and I wasn't here." He shakes his head. "I ran. I ran to escape my feelings. Your world fell apart, and I was overseas. I wasn't here to celebrate with my family when you found out you were pregnant. I wasn't here when Carter had his accident, and I wasn't here when your already broken heart was pulled, still beating, from your chest as you learned your infant, your baby, suffered from leukemia.

"I can never forgive myself for running, for placing so many miles between myself and those I hold dear. I'm sorry, and I will spend the rest of my life attempting to be the man I should have been when you needed me the most. I stand before you, your best friend, your brother-in-law, and plead that you will consider allowing me to give Ian and you this chance."

"Stop," I plead, my hand out between us.

He responds by placing his index finger in front of my mouth. "Don't speak. Give it thought tonight. Go upstairs and make your pros-and-cons list. Then we will talk about it tomorrow."

I'm dumbfounded, totally at a loss for words, and I'm insulted by his comment about my tendency to make pros-and-cons lists. I hate that he knows me that well. In fact, I believe he knows me better than his brother ever did. Lewis and I are alike in that we are Type A personalities; we like lists, strive for goals, and crave order. Carter was a go-with-the-flow, always-land-on-his-feet type of person. Everyone said we were living proof that opposites do attract.

Through my tears, I see Lewis's blurry silhouette kneeling before me. This strong, intelligent man is humbled at my feet, broken down to his soul in front of me. *I can consider his offer; I can do this for him. I owe it to Ian to investigate every alternative, no matter how scandalous it sounds.*

I nod, unable to vocalize my understanding of his plea. I vow that I will allow him this opportunity. I nod again and scurry to the safety of my bedroom.

I ensure Ian's monitor is on and the sound is up before I pace. I pace from my bedroom door to the window then back again. I pace, unaware that I'm doing so. I pace, and I process the revelation, the confession that I witnessed in the kitchen mere moments ago.

Lewis, my long-time best friend, humbly spilled his feelings onto the long-overdue-for-a-mopping linoleum floor before me. He threw me a life raft, a lifeline for Ian. He's offering me that which I've mourned along with the passing of my husband. *Hope.*

It's a tiny flicker, a barely-there light, but it's lit. It's lit, and my heart rate speeds at the implications. *Hope.* Hope that's eluded me for far too many months is now placed at my feet. *Will I cling to it? Hell yeah, I will!* I vowed long ago to never stop looking, to never stop researching… Lewis brings with him hope—hope for my son and hope for me.

My mind reels with possibilities, logistics, ramifications, and what ifs. I'm giddy and horrified. This decision, this act, might save my son's life, and it could forever place a scarlet letter upon my breast. Lewis's idea—this crazy, far-fetched, last straw effort—could just be the one to ease my son's suffering and save his life.

My hands tremble as I pull a notebook and pen from my bedside table. *Pros and cons. Pros and cons.* The tiny flame of hope urges me to start positive. I write "Pros" at the top of the page.

<u>Pros</u>:

Ian lives
Ian is in remission
Ian is healthy
I've lost my husband but still have our son
My world continues to spin for many more trips around the sun

The pen in hand, I pause at the top of the next column on this sheet of paper. I hesitate because I don't want to brainstorm ways to talk myself out of this. I want to do this for my son; I must try everything.

<u>Cons:</u>
Half-sibling is not a match
Ian becomes too sick before baby is born
Ian rejects the donor cells
I miscarry
I will be pregnant with my brother-in-law's child
Ian's half-sibling will be his cousin
Our family tree will be straight, lacking branches
Gossip
Lewis will feel obligated to me and our baby, even as he falls in love and marries the woman he deserves
I will be a widow with two children under three

9
LEWIS

The Next Morning

I've had many long nights, but this one seems the longest. I look at my cell phone once again to find it's six. I can't lay here another minute. I swing my legs over the side of the bed, scrunching my toes in the area rug beneath.

My exhausted mind awaits Ryan's choice. I've tried to come up with every possible con she may list. *I'm keeping my promise to my brother. I must take care of Ian and Ryan. I must do everything in my power. Anything and everything. We have to try, for Ian's sake.*

I quietly make my way to the kitchen, deciding to surprise Ryan by making breakfast. I carefully pull out the eggs, pancake mix, bacon, and the frozen orange juice concentrate.

I get out the measuring cups, mixing bowls, mixer, blender, and utensils next. With the entire countertop covered, I realize this kitchen is much too small. *She needs a bigger place*; I'll save that discussion for another day. *One thing at a time.*

I warm the griddle and frying pan while I prepare the batter by hand. I pour two pancakes onto the griddle then line up the bacon in the cast-iron skillet.

Oh! Chocolate chips. Ian would love them with his pancake. I grab them and some fresh strawberries from the fridge. I rinse then slice the berries as

I monitor the pancakes and bacon. I place finished food in the warmer and start a new batch of each. I plop the frozen juice concentrate in the blender with water; I'll wait until Ryan wakes to turn it on.

Bacon works every time. Soon, Ryan follows its scent toward me.

"Mornin'," she mumbles behind me.

I spin to find her yawning, leaning against the small island, her hair a mess. She's swimming in one of Carter's old t-shirts. Clearly, she experienced a long night, too. This reminds me of the morning after one of our dead-week parties in college, and I fight a grin.

"I've made pancakes," I announce proudly. "Go get Ian."

"He's up," she growls. "Can I have coffee?"

Crap! Coffee. How could I forget her coffee?

"I'll put some on," I promise.

"Fine," she pouts, stomping down the hallway.

Way to go, idiot. Coffee is the most important part of breakfast this early, and I forgot it.

I switch the blender on then start her coffee maker. When I turn the blender off, I stand at the doorway to the hallway to listen. I can hear Ryan talking to Ian as she changes his clothes and administers his medicine.

Remembering the food, I jog to the stovetop. Luckily, I haven't burned it. I flip the pancakes then the bacon before I pour juice into the glasses and Ian's sippy cup.

Ian waves when Ryan carries him to his highchair.

"Good morning, buddy," I greet, holding my hand out for a high five. When he complies, I tell him, "I made you a very special pancake."

He claps his hands in front of him before I return to the stove. I pull two silver dollar-sized pancakes from the griddle, pour a few chocolate chips on the plate, cut the pancake into bite-sized portions, then decorate the other side of the plate with sliced strawberries before placing it on the tray in front of Ian.

While I watch him struggle to grip a bright berry then raise it to his mouth, Ryan fixes her plate behind me. Although my attention is on my nephew, I am acutely aware of her movements mere feet away.

Ian lifts a strawberry, extending it towards me. I lean forward, open my mouth, and allow him to shove the berry in. I make a big production of chewing. "Yum, yum, yum," I mumble while chewing. When he extends another, I guide his hand towards his own mouth.

Ryan slides a plate beside me on the table before taking her seat across from us. I notice that my plate is full, while hers contains only bacon and strawberries.

At my arched eyebrow, she explains, "Too many carbs in pancakes and syrup. I need to catch up on work, not fit in a workout today."

I want to argue she's a bit thin. The past year's stress shows. I want to tell her she's beautiful, and there's no need to concern herself with a few pounds. I want to chastise her, but I don't.

Ryan

"So, let me have it. Pros first," Lewis states between bites of syrup-bathed pancake. "Want me to go get your notebook?"

I shake my head, leaning to one side and pulling my folded list from the pocket of my pajama pants. I'd hoped to drown myself in 2 to three cups of coffee prior to this conversation; I feel I'm entering it ill-equipped.

My fingers fumble as the tattered paper fights my attempts to flatten it. I reach across it, snag my mug, and allow the coffee flavor to warm me. I fear even an intravenous dose of coffee would not have me ready for this. I contemplate passing the note to him but decide I'm an adult and need to tackle this task as one.

"Pros," I begin, my voice shaky. "Ian's healthy." I look up through my lashes at Lewis.

His eyes are not on me, instead watching Ian as he sits in his highchair. After spending most of his nephew's life abroad, Lewis enjoys every moment with him.

"That is the entire reason for my suggestion," he states, moving his warm blue eyes to me.

His sincerity brings tears to my eyes. Lewis extends his arm across the table to cover mine. When he gives it a gentle squeeze, I will my eyes to look back at him.

"May I?" he asks, tugging the corner of my paper.

I lift my arm, allowing him to pull it across the table. I dare not breathe or move for that matter. I'm frozen, anticipation and fear warring within me.

While he reads, Lewis nods then raises an eyebrow. He taps his fingers on the corner of my notebook paper for a moment then slides the list in my direction.

"While there are more cons on your list than pros," he begins, eyes piercing mine, "Ian's health is much more than one pro."

I nod.

"Now, as for the cons... I've spent hours now, reading on the subject." Lewis takes a sip of his orange juice then continues. "The science they use in the in-vitro process selects only those embryos that, while healthy, are also an HCL match."

My eyes widen at his statement. He, Ian's uncle, conducted research on this topic, while I, Ian's mother, have not.

"I'm not going anywhere," he states, not for the first time. "As I've said before, I plan to be close to help with Ian. I'm not going anywhere."

His eyes implore mine to grasp this once and for all.

"You won't be alone during the pregnancy. As for the rest, it doesn't matter what anyone else thinks." He draws in a quick breath. "All that matters is Ian's health and what the two of us think." His index finger points back and forth between us.

"It will not be a second child with no husband and support," he continues. "I will be here every step of the way for 18 years and beyond. Who cares if our child would be both a brother and cousin to Ian? Who cares if you have a child with your brother-in-law?" He sucks in a long, audible breath through his nose while gathering his thoughts. "It doesn't matter what 'they' think. We are the *only* family either of us have left. I can't lose my nephew after losing my brother. We have to try *everything*! He's so little; it's unfair."

I spy hints of tears in his sky-blue eyes.

"We have to try," he pleads. "Karma owes you. Our baby will be a match." Again, his finger ping pongs between us. "You have my vow to help, for nine months and beyond, as the baby's father and as Ian's uncle. I will be involved; I will not leave any of you."

Lewis leaves his chair, squatting beside me as I sit. "You are my best friend." He looks to Ian then back to me. "With Mom unable to recognize me most days, you are the only family I have left."

Ryan

. . .

While Lewis and Ian take care of the breakfast dishes, I return to my room, in need of a shower. I sit on the end of my unmade bed, my mind reeling from this morning's declarations.

Lewis on his knees strips me of my will to argue. Lewis on his knees, declaring I'm the only family he has left, breaks my heart. Lewis on his knees, stating I'm still his best friend, warms my belly. Gradually, that warmth spreads, driving out the fear.

He's addressed every one of my arguments; he had an answer for them all. This man, Carter's twin and my best friend, vows to support Ian and me forever. He longs to have a child with me in hopes of healing Ian. Knowing him as well as I do, I have no doubt he's sincere in his promise to remain close, assist, and support the two of us.

Three.

The three of us.

We're really going to do this. We're going to a lab to create a child to save Ian. We're going to tangle ourselves together for years to come. We're going to create a life, a sibling to Ian, a child that will ensure my best friend will always be by my side.

Damn them if they judge us. Damn them if they gossip. God forbid, if they were in our shoes, they would stop at nothing to save their child, just as we are. Parents sacrifice. Parents love unconditionally. Parents do everything in their power to protect their children.

As Lewis said, karma owes us.

We have to try.

In the shower, my mind moves 100 miles a minute. Lewis plans to live with us, so I need to redecorate the guest room to make it his room. I'll need boxes for the trinkets and to clean out the closet.

The closet.

Carter's items are in that closet.

I couldn't part with everything. *I'm still not ready.*

Tears well as I remember how difficult it was to pack after he passed. *I felt so alone.* Lewis was in Dubai, my mother-in-law was in the nursing home, and Ian was too young to be of any assistance.

It took me two months to even consider moving his belongings. Ian turned ill, and I couldn't sleep. I moved his clothes to the spare closet, still on hangers, and I cried all night.

A burning pain returns to my chest, and every breath I take fuels the fire.

He's gone. He's gone, and Ian's sick; I can't lose him, too.

I fall to the shower floor. The warm spray feels like needles upon my skin.

Carter's gone.

I can't fight the pain. Under the sounds of the shower, I weep.

10

LEWIS

That Evening

As Ryan feeds Ian his pasta, I notice her glances at my notebook in the center of the table. I bite my lips to avoid a sly grin. I purposely placed my notebook there before I set the table; I knew it would pique her curiosity. I asked her earlier today if we could talk after dinner tonight, and she stated Ian would skip his bath, allowing us more time to chat. So, she knows the topic of our conversation hides inside its pages, lying mere inches from her.

Neither of us say a word as she tucks Ian into bed, and I load the dishwasher. She wipes down the counters and table, taking great care not to disturb my notebook.

Needing to transition from silence into our discussion, I offer, "Let's have a drink. Wine?"

She nods, still silent, and I now regret tormenting her with my notebook. I may have set myself up for a difficult time. She pulls a new bottle of wine from the refrigerator door while I place two wine glasses on the table.

"Will I need paper and pen?" she asks once I pour the chardonnay.

"Nope," I answer, popping the "P."

She quirks a brow at my light mood.

"I brought some talking points and research to share with you," I admit, patting the notebook cover with my open hand.

"Let's have it," she urges, taking a sip of wine.

I make a production of opening my notebook to my outline before I take a long drink of wine. "This would have tasted great with the pasta tonight," I share.

She nods nervously.

"I have two topics for us," I start, her eyes on me. "Which do you want first? 'A' or 'B'?"

She rolls her eyes at my shenanigans. "Oh, my god! Start already."

"Okay. Okay," I placate, palms to her in surrender. "'A' it is then. Baby making."

She spews out a mouthful of wine before she can swallow, bathing the table and my notebook paper with droplets.

Coughing and laughing, she informs me, "You can't just drop a topic that big by blurting it."

I chuckle. "You knew we'd need to talk about it sooner or later," I tease.

"I have wine up my nostrils," she laughs, and I join her.

"I've listed a few items we need to address. Some must be completed in order; others don't," I share. "We'll need to visit the clinic. I'll need to give a sample to check that my swimmers are of Olympic quality, and you'll need to stop using birth control."

Ryan's eyes widen and her lips form an "O."

"I'm…" She stammers. "I'm not taking any."

Wow. I just now realized how personal that topic is. I have no doubt she's been with no one since Carter's passing. When I wrote the words on my list, it didn't register. However, now, it's information Ryan's brother-in-law shouldn't know.

"After… Well, you know…" she explains. "I was so out of it, I didn't take my pills. Once I realized I'd missed weeks worth of them, I decided I really had no reason to keep taking them." She shrugs, quirking her mouth to the side.

Hands up, palms to her, I apologize. "I'm sorry. I don't mean to pry."

Again, she shrugs. "At least we won't delay a month for my body to adjust to not taking the pills."

Nervous, I move on. "I'm paying for the procedures as I don't think health insurance covers this, and in-vitro is expensive."

She opens her mouth to argue but I cut her off. "I promised my brother I'd take care of you and Ian."

"I can't let you pay for all of it," she argues. "When we know the amount, I'll pay my part."

"Ryan, it's over 10 thousand dollars per month," I inform. "There's medication, the procedure, and the genetic screenings we have to ask for, too."

"I still need to contribute," she challenges, face turning red.

"So, the second topic is finances," I announce, quickly moving on to the topic she'll fight me on. "I made a vow at my brother's funeral that I would care for you and Ian in his absence. I'm not sure if he ever told you, but I made good money. *Really* good money."

She stares at me, eyes assessing.

Feeling she needs more information, I explain. "Hell, I've listed my apartment in Kansas City for just under a million dollars. I've plenty of money for the three of us."

Her squinty eyes, red face, and pursed lips send me the message. She's not pleased with my statement.

11

RYAN

Later

I see red. *Who does he think he is?* I may not be wealthy, but I have money. Sure, Ian's hospital bills are quickly chipping away at my reserves, but I make a decent wage. I need to set him straight.

"It's my turn to talk," I announce. "So, no interruptions." I point sternly at him. "The house is paid off. I used most of Carter's life insurance to pay off our mortgage and the car and tucked the rest away for emergencies. I negotiated working from home so I could keep our health insurance, and given Ian's illness, it's a good thing I did. Now, it doesn't cover 100 percent, but it covers most of the medical expenses."

"Why make this difficult?" he has the nerve to ask. "I've saved enough that I can live off the interest for most of my life. I don't have children, parents, a wife, or a girlfriend to spend it on. This isn't charity or pity. This is your best friend and brother-in-law keeping a promise to your late husband. Fight it all you want; I'm paying for the procedure."

Smug, he sits there, arms crossed, informing me I have no say in this. *Pompous ass.*

"This house is too small," he blurts. "It will make for tight quarters if you squeeze a newborn in with the three of us. You need a bigger house, and I can make that happen."

The nerve. He's not Oprah. He can't simply gift me a house.

"I can hear the cogs spinning," he teases, pointing to my head. "The way I figure it, I can buy me a place nearby and constantly visit you and the kids, or I can purchase a bigger house for the four of us to enjoy."

"You make it sound simple," I bite.

He smirks again. The man *actually* smirks at me. If he wasn't Ian's uncle, I'd throw his smug ass out right now.

"See, that's what you aren't getting," he states.

I'm not going to sit here and let him call me stupid. I push my chair back, preparing to leave.

"I can pay cash for a house today," he shares, furthering his point. "I need real estate to invest in. We're living on top of each other here, and don't get me started on how tiny your kitchen is."

He's right, and it hurts. With Carter's construction work ebbing and flowing with the seasons and housing market, this tiny, two-bedroom with a detached garage was all we could afford. We bought it with the hope of adding on to the back as our family grew over the years. It's not much, but Carter bought it with me. We were two young kids, ready to take on the world. Heck, we even struggled the first year with making the monthly payment.

"Ry?" Lewis seeks my attention.

He's not fighting fair. He knows I love when he calls me "Ry" like he did in college. It warms me to my soul.

"Please don't fight me on this. I have the means to lighten some of your obligations, so let me. Carter never intended for you to be doing all of this on your own. As Ian's godfather, I promised to care for him if something happened to the two of you. Something did happen, so allow me to help."

I hate that he is right. I hate needing help. He did promise Carter and me that he would step up in our absence to care for Ian. It makes sense that he feels he should help now. If Ian weren't sick, I'd be able to care for us easily. If Carter weren't gone, we'd have enough. We wouldn't live flashy and would budget to afford many things, but we'd be happy and get by. I hate the "if" game.

"We need to set some ground rules," I murmur, barely above a whisper.

He nods after finishing his glass of wine. Rising, he refills his and tops off my glass.

"Ours is not a typical household. If we were a married couple, I'd pay the bills. I want to pay for half of the utilities," he demands.

I open my lips to protest.

"Wait," he urges. "I'm compromising. I *want* to pay *all* of the bills." His smile is sincere. "I'm living here and conducting my business here, so I need to contribute."

When I don't verbally object, he continues. "What do you think it will take, a month or two to get pregnant?"

I scoff. "Some couples try for years without conceiving."

"Oh. So, six months to a year?" he counters, worry growing on his face.

I shrug. I don't share that Carter and I got pregnant the first month we tried when I quit taking the pill. I'm not eager to put that pressure on top of all we already have. Both of us are very aware that time is the enemy.

"I hate to put it off too long," Lewis's words cut into my thoughts. "Ian needs a transplant ASAP, and you'd be pregnant for nine months after we conceive. It's for his sake we need to hurry."

I tilt my head, realizing he has a notebook but only two topics to discuss.

"What?" he asks.

I shake my head.

"Uh-huh," he argues. "Something's going on in there." He points to my head.

It's annoying how well he knows me. He remembers too much from our college years.

"Did you need a notebook to discuss in-vitro and finances?" I smile, pointing to his open notebook in front of him.

He looks down, turning through several pages.

"I've done a lot of research and taken notes," he informs. "I had several items on my outlines."

"Like?" I prod.

"Well, a more in-depth discussion of your birth control methods and research on how long to wait after discontinuing each before attempting a pregnancy," he chuckles. "I could teach a birth control class with all the different types I learned about."

I can't help but laugh at the image of him, late at night, researching and taking notes with his laptop. I laugh so hard I snort.

He smirks. "Very ladylike."

This elicits another snort and extends my laughter.

"I'm glad you find this hilarious," he chides, fighting a smile. "I also have a counterpoint for all of the cons I thought you might throw at me."

"Maybe I'm not as predictable as you'd like to believe," I sassily throw in his direction.

"In the six years I've known you," he chuckles, "you've only surprised me twice."

I jerk my head back at his statement. *That can't be right.* I chew on my tongue as I surf through all our memories for the two times he might mean. *I'm not predictable. Well, I'm not predictable all the time; sometimes, I'm spontaneous. Hmm.*

"I'll put you out of your misery," he offers, a wide smile present on his face. "The night during senior year that you stayed up partying before your last final…"

"That one even surprised me," I admit. "What was I thinking? And the second?"

His tongue darts out to wet his lower lip, followed by his teeth tugging at it in contemplation. His eyes ping pong between mine. I brace myself, pouring another glass of wine to prepare for his next proclamation.

"When you went with my brother on a date," he states, eyes challenging me to react.

Why would dating his brother have caught him off guard? I dated, and he knew I dated. Is it the fact that Carter seemed the opposite of me? Lewis and I are so alike, and we became instant friends. *If he knew me so well, why did dating Carter surprise him?*

12

RYAN

Later

Later that night, I lie in bed, my mind reeling with all the topics of the past 48 hours. After an hour of attempting to dissect Lewis's surprise that I dated his brother, I choose to set that nugget aside.

I've agreed to get pregnant with my brother-in-law's child. I roll my eyes. I can already hear the whispers spreading as my baby bump swells. Add to that the controversy surrounding savior babies, and we set ourselves up for public scrutiny. It's probably a good thing that, after Carter's death, my friends distanced themselves from me. Odd that I haven't realized I'm lacking in the friend department until tonight. Lewis remains my closest friend.

Pushing all of that aside, a glimmer of hope grows low in my belly. Well, it was a glimmer when Lewis first suggested it. Now, it's a blossom of hope. I'm unsure how this will all work out, but for the first time since Ian's diagnosis, I have hope for a cure. I'm a realist, too, however. Lewis shared the success percentage, and while it's not spectacular, I have far more hope than I had a week ago.

For months, I've been lost as there had been nothing I could do to save my son. I hit rock bottom when no donors matched. Like Lewis, I'm a control freak. I'm a planner, and I'm a doer. When it comes to the health of a family member, there is no control. The plan to conceive a baby with Lewis gives me a bit of control back.

I stare out my window into the darkness of the backyard. I wonder if I will get pregnant the first month we try like I did with Carter. A pregnancy takes 40 weeks. Add to that the time it takes to get pregnant, and we're looking at a year as the soonest we might help Ian. That's a long time, but it's our best chance. The wait time for this plan to work out is maddening.

I can't do anything tonight, so I might as well go to sleep. If only it were that simple. I hate sleeping alone.

"Ahh…" I groan out loud. I pound my fist into my pillow, trying to assume a comfortable position. I flip from my left side to my right, pulling the pillow from the empty side of the bed to cuddle into my chest.

Why would Lewis be surprised that I dated his brother? He was and still is my best friend. *Should I have asked his permission? Is that why he was shocked? Or is it the fact they are identical twins? Did he think that, in dating his brother, it was kind of like dating him?*

Thinking back, I try to remember how Lewis acted as Carter and I began dating. I didn't notice a difference in our friendship; we even hung out as a threesome several times. Tomorrow, I'll ask him what surprised him. I need to know.

13

RYAN

Days Later

Each day, I thank God that Lewis returned to assist me with Ian. Before he moved in, the only interactions I had were with Ian, doctors, and nurses. They suggested I attend support groups, but I had no one to care for Ian and couldn't risk exposing him to germs if he attended with me.

Now, I enjoy outings like the grocery store and my online support groups. Before, my only free moments were while Ian slept; I was never more than a few feet away either, even in his slumber. Now, I focus on my work in the new office and complete my assignments ahead of my deadlines. I actually enjoy my work instead of stressing over it.

I feel I have more patience with Ian because I spend time away. He can't help it that he whines when he doesn't feel good, and I hate that, at times, I had a short temper.

I missed Lewis while he was away; I missed my best friend. With the time difference, my emails waited hours and sometimes days for his reply. It was worse after Carter's accident. Without his daily conversations, I relied more on responses from Lewis. I found myself utterly alone, starving for adult interaction. I emailed him daily, and he responded most days.

I talked out loud to Ian, even though he could only babble in return. On days he spent in the hospital, I often talked to the nurses whenever possible.

Eventually, some of them took their breaks in Ian's room to keep me company. I know they pitied me, and I appreciate that they went out of their way to give me what I needed.

With Lewis in my life, I miss Carter even more. I spend my days staring at his identical twin, his brother, and he makes me long for my husband. I miss his touch, his voice, his humor, and most of all, his warm body in bed next to mine. For a while, I slept with Ian in my bed, hoping he'd cure my loneliness. It didn't work. I found I slept less with him in my bed as I strained to listen to his every breath. It wasn't fair of me to keep him so close, so I ended it before it developed into a habit.

After that, I spent many nights sleeping on the floor outside his room. At least on the floor, I didn't have memories of Carter, and I felt a little less lonely.

14

LEWIS

The Next Night

A wailing sound cuts through my playtime with Ian. I place him in his playpen before striding down the short hall to investigate. Outside the bathroom door, I place my ear near the wood, just as a muted wail sounds. Pausing for a moment with my hand on the knob, I listen to Ryan's sobs echoing in the shower stall. I don't hesitate any longer, and I open the door.

"Ry?" I call, unsure what might be wrong. "Honey, are you okay?"

After loud sniffles, she responds, "I'm fine."

Fine. Fine? I learned long ago that "fine" is never fine with a lady. Giving it no thought, I push the door open, stepping inside. Having not thought this through, I now stand staring at Ryan who is naked and curled up in the bottom of the shower.

Moments pass before I snap out of my stupor. I snag her robe from the nearby hook, turn off the water, then wrap her up. In her current position, the robe does little to cover her. Bending down, I scoop her up, carrying her into the bedroom. I crawl onto the comforter, cuddling her to me. My hands caress her hair and shoulders.

"Shh," I plead. "Shh. You're okay; Ian's okay. Everything's okay."

Her sobs subside and sniffles continue. Holding her tightly in my arms, her body curled into mine, I realize all the items I can't control. When I returned, I focused on supporting Ryan emotionally, helping her around the house, and watching Ian to give her free time. I thought I had it all under control for her. I'm just now realizing I held a false sense of security.

Try as I might, I can't erase Carter's loss or Ian's illness. The looming dangers ahead for Ian overshadow everything. I can't erase her pain; I can only offer her support. I can't cure Ian; I can only try to help. All my money won't make the pain or fear disappear.

"I'm sorry," Ryan sniffles.

"Shh," I soothe. "It's okay."

"I..." She hiccups. "I...uh..." She wipes her cheeks with the end of her terry cloth robe. "I... I need to..."

Her words hang heavy as I wait to find out what's upset her. I tuck her hair behind her ear as I crane my neck to see her face.

"You'll be staying..." She hiccups.

"Yes. I'm not going anywhere," I restate.

"Need to clean out your closet..." she states.

"Okay. I can help with that," I offer, unsure why that brought on tears.

"Carter's stuff is in there," she whispers.

There. That's the reason for her crying in my arms. I tighten my hold on her, hoping she understands she's not alone.

"I'll do whatever you ask," I promise. "There's room in the storage area above the garage or even in the office closet."

She nods.

"I just couldn't bear donating everything," she whispers.

"You don't ever have to do that," I whisper back. "We can keep his memories."

Again, she nods.

"I miss him so much," she murmurs, her words stifling in the silence.

"I know."

"I'll always miss him," she whispers.

"He was your husband. You have every right to miss him," I affirm.

She wiggles to reposition the robe to cover her legs. I'm very aware of her naked presence and how inappropriate it is given our topic of conversation.

"I should go check on Ian," I say, pulling my arm from under her and sliding off her bed.

Suddenly aware of her nudity, she scrambles to slip her arms in and tie her robe. I notice her cheeks pinkening as I pull her bedroom door closed behind me.

15

RYAN

Days Later

I'm a woman on a mission. I didn't sleep well as thoughts of Lewis's admission of surprise at my dating Carter still haunt me, as does the mystery of the woman he traveled halfway around the world to avoid.

I ate a protein bar for breakfast at my desk, and I have another for lunch while Lewis plays with Ian in the house. I complete six projects before I call it a day and join the boys in the house.

Inside the house, Lewis insists I play with Ian while he grills pork chops and baked potatoes. I'm not sure what the boys did all day while I worked, but Ian nearly falls asleep rolling a car back and forth with me on the floor.

"Dinner's ready," Lewis proudly announces, carrying food to the table. "Ian, time to eat."

As if he understands all that Lewis says, Ian crawls to the kitchen. I secure him in his highchair and tie a bib around his neck. Ready for food, Ian claps excitedly.

"Here you go," Lewis states, sliding diced hotdog onto Ian's tray.

"And for you," he says, sliding a plate in front of me.

"This looks delicious," I croon, fork and knife cutting into the pork chop. "A girl could get used to this," I say, marveling that my baked potato swims in melted butter while wearing bacon bits.

Lewis pauses mid-step, plate in hand, staring at me. I tilt my head to the side, wondering what I said that caused him to pause. I run my words back through my head. I can't find offense in any of them. After a moment, he takes his seat across from me, a sweet smile upon his face.

"So..." I decide to find my answers, starting now. "Tell me more about your mystery woman."

He freezes, fork inches from his mouth. His eyes the size of saucers, he places his fork back onto his plate.

"What brought this on?" he asks, affronted.

"This did," I state, motioning to my plate. "You didn't just grill. You fixed my baked potato. She'd be a lucky girl to have you around."

Lewis's face twists into a scowl. Not the reaction I thought he'd have about this woman he supposedly is head over heels for.

"I told you, it wouldn't work," he growls. "This isn't something I want to talk about."

"Help me understand," I plead. "All I know is you really liked the woman, and you left the country because you couldn't have her."

He lets out a long exhale, placing both forearms on the table at the side of his plate. He closes his eyes for a moment before resting his forehead on his steepled hands.

"It's nothing really," he murmurs.

"I call B.S.," I argue. "As your best friend, I know you wouldn't leave your family and move to another country if it was *nothing*."

"As my best friend, you should trust me," he counters.

"Trust you?" I scoff. "I've always trusted you. Heck, right now, I'm trusting you to care for Ian while I work."

"I'm his uncle. It's not a hardship," he spits.

"Easy," I chide. "I'm just trying to understand."

"What's there to understand? The relationship wasn't meant to be, so I took the high road and removed myself from the situation."

I turn his words over in my mind. A relationship that wasn't meant to be...*Why?*

"Help me understand," I beg. "Was she your boss, or were you her boss?"

He shakes his head at me. "She wasn't single, so I stepped aside."

Wow. I reach my arm out to place my hand on top of his. *He loved this woman.* Heck, he probably *still* loves this woman. Instead of following through on his feelings, he took the high road and removed himself from the situation. My heart breaks for him. I squeeze his hand.

"Thank you," I whisper, ashamed that I brought it up. It's easy to see he's still pained at the thought of her.

He slides his hand from mine, taking a bite of his pork chop. I follow his lead, enjoying my dinner. Out the side of my eye, I notice Ian isn't moving. He's asleep; his little head tips to the side.

"Lewis," I whisper.

He looks to me, dread on his face. He thinks I plan to talk more about the woman.

I tilt my head in Ian's direction. "What did the two of you do today?"

Lewis shrugs. "The usual. We played, and we napped."

Worry creeps up my spine. *What if he's caught something? What if he's getting worse?*

Sensing my unease, Lewis offers support. "I'm sure his nap was short, and we played hard. That's all."

He rises, extricates Ian from the highchair, and carries him to bed. My heavy heart aches. Lewis stepping up to help in every way he can means the world to me. With each passing day, I feel less overwhelmed. His time with Ian allows me to relax, regroup, work, and attend online group meetings. This man lost his twin when I lost my husband, he's in love with a woman he can't be with, and he's supporting me in every way he can.

I sip my water slowly, my thoughts swimming with so many topics right now. I carry both our plates to the sink, deciding to drop my questioning. I've pried enough for today.

Ryan

"Good morning," I greet, entering the kitchen the next day. I'm sure I look like crap; I didn't get much sleep. "I love the smell of bacon." I tell him something he's very aware of.

"You like the taste of bacon, too," he reminds me. "How would you like your eggs?"

"I'm not in the mood," I inform. "Bacon sounds good, though."

He leaves the sizzling bacon, turning to face me across the island, leaning on his forearms. "You need your strength for Ian. You need something more than bacon."

While I'm in no mood for eggs and have little appetite, I'm not in the mood to argue.

"Fried," I mumble.

"Coming right up," he promises me cheerily.

I rest my chin in my hands, my elbows propped on the counter, turning to watch Ian playing with his toys on the nearby throw rug. At least one of us slept last night.

I jump when Lewis's hand appears on my shoulder, his arm around my back, and he places a kiss to the crown of my head.

"We might all need to nap this afternoon," his low voice murmurs near my ear.

My shoulder feels his hot touch long after he returns to the stove and frying pans. I was startled because he surprised me, not because of his touch. I've come to like his touch, and I look forward to it.

"Are you okay?" His voice snaps me out of my own head.

"Just tired. That's all," I vow. "I may need to join Ian for his morning *and* afternoon naps today."

"Even if you don't fall asleep, the pregnancy books state resting is important for you and our future baby." I note the pride in Lewis's smile. He's really getting into learning all he can about pregnancy; he doesn't want any surprises.

"I'm not pregnant yet," I remind him.

"I read it doesn't hurt to be prepared," he shares, turning back to the food. "Mothers are more tired in second pregnancies as they have little ones to chase around, and they didn't during the first one."

That makes sense. In the months to come, I should reread the book I loaned to him.

"We can take turns reading chapters in the pregnancy book if you'd like." He sneaks a quick look over his shoulder then begins plating our breakfast.

We're thinking alike again; it's crazy how that happens. In college, our friends and study buddies would tease us endlessly about finishing each other's sentences. They called us the old married couple. I shake my head.

"What?" he asks, sliding a plate of much too much bacon and fried egg in front of me.

"Nothing," I lie, too exhausted to share.

He pops a piece of bacon off my plate into his mouth then joins me on a stool at the island. I smile as he has not filled a plate for himself. I guess he plans to share with me. When his hand reaches in for the next strip of bacon, he leans his face close to mine. I turn to face him, our noses nearly touching. I chew on my lip, wondering what he's thinking.

He places a kiss to the tip of my nose, which is a first. Then, he sneaks his empty hand around my back to snag another piece of bacon from my other side.

So, the tip of the nose kiss was a distraction; he's good.

16

LEWIS

Late that Night

She's like a dog with a bone. The lights above the kitchen island feel like heat lamps under her squinted eyes.

"I don't understand why you will not tell me," she continues. "It's not like I know her or will ever bump into her. Perhaps telling me will help you move on once and for all."

She leans back on her stool, arms folded across her chest, one eyebrow raised in my direction.

"Moonlighting with the CIA, are you?" I ask. "I've shared all I plan to share, so take what you got and be happy with it."

"I don't accept defeat," she declares.

"Oh, believe me, I know that." I scoff, remembering many times in the years I've known her that she never gave up.

"Did you tell Carter all about her before you left for Dubai?" Ryan asks.

Direct hit to the gut. Her words cut me to the core. Her face informs me she knows I did, and she's hurt I wouldn't also share with her. I can't be the one to upset her.

I let out a long, audible breath. "I'll allow you ten questions. You may ask only ten, and I can refuse four of them if I choose."

She cocks her head to the side, assessing my offer, no doubt trying to find any loopholes in it. She nods, resituating herself again. As her eyes look upward in thought, she purses her lips.

"Question one." She grins, feeling as though she's about to break me.

I have no plans to divulge every detail, but she doesn't need to know that. I'll let her have her fun interrogating me while remaining vague.

She wears a proud smirk. "Do you love her?"

Damn. She's going straight for the jugular. I'm not surprised; I thought she'd work her way up to the big questions. *Should I answer this one or refuse?* If this is her starting point, I will need to pass on others down the line. Answering this one doesn't allude to the identity. So, I nod, leaning my forearms on the counter between us and bracing myself for her next inquiry.

"Wow!" She shakes her head. "I expected you to pass on that answer. You still love her. Hmmm. Number two: Have you been in contact with her since you returned to the U.S.?" Her fingers strum on the countertop, awaiting my answer.

"Pass." Answering this will only double her efforts in the investigation.

"Three," she grumbles, upset to be denied. "Do I know her?"

"Pass." I detest the venom I hear in my voice.

"Are you sure?" she taunts. "That only leaves you with two more passes."

I nod, regretting my starting this game in the first place.

"Question four: Is she still married?"

Think. Think. Think. I need to answer this one. I place my head in my hands, elbows remaining on the counter. "Sort of," I mumble.

I can hear the gears in her brain turning on that one. I didn't promise to give clear answers to the questions. I just won't lie.

"How can someone be 'sort of' married? I mean, is she divorced or separated?"

"Are those your fifth and sixth questions?" I taunt, avoiding further details.

She shakes her head, mumbling, "Sort of married, still in love with her, won't tell me if I know her or if he's seen her recently." Her teeth tug repeatedly on her lower lip in frustration.

"Fine," she sighs. "Question five: Does she know you love her?"

I shake my head.

"Do you plan to tell her how you feel?" Her words come quicker as she tries to trick me.

I shrug.

"You have to answer," she states, raising her voice.

"My answer is I. Don't. Know." I spit. It's the truth. I think I know, but I'm not 100 percent sure.

"I should have known you weren't going to answer my questions. I never should have been sucked into your little game." She pushes her stool back, arms angrily clinched across her chest.

"Question seven: You claim you went to Dubai to get her off your mind since she wasn't available. Did you let her know how you felt verbally or physically before you ran?"

"First, I didn't run," I bite. Instantly, I'm angry at myself. It's a lie; I ran. I ran and hid. It's the only way I could… "Second, no."

"Hmm," she tilts her head to the side, pondering my answer. "So, you love this woman, but you've never acted upon it and chose to leave the country to keep from messing around with her because she's married?"

"Yes," I reply with a smirk. She burned another question there that she's not aware of. I have two passes left for her remaining two questions. I can see the light at the end of the tunnel.

"If you had it to do all over again, would you tell her how you feel?" She leans forward, interest peaked.

I nod.

Her face lights up and eyes widen. She loves this juicy bit of knowledge.

"Would I like her?" she asks.

"Yes," I answer. "You'd like her a lot. There. That was your ten questions."

She shakes her head, eyes peering at me, ready to argue.

"After seven, you restated my previous answers in the form of a question, and I replied 'yes.'" I smile, victorious. As she's still shaking her head, I explain. "You said, and I quote, 'So, you love this woman, but you've never acted upon it and chose to leave the country to keep from messing around with her because she's married?' And I answered that question."

"Not fair!" she argues.

"I answered eight of your ten questions," I remind her. "That's two more than I *had* to answer." I shrug.

"Humph." Her chest rises as though she's about to argue then falls in defeat. "The only thing I learned is that you love her."

I lift my chin, my eyes remaining on hers. *Why does admitting I'm in love with the woman make me feel weak, like less of a man? Is it because it's pathetic that I love a woman I can't have?* I let out a long sigh.

"I'm calling it a night," I say, rising from my stool.

Ryan follows my lead. "Lewis?" she calls to me before I enter the hall.

I turn to face her, my hand upon the wall.

"It can't be easy to love her and not act upon it." Her face softens. "You tried the whole 'leaving the country for two years to move on' thing, and that didn't work. My advice is you should tell her how you feel. Don't physically do it, just tell her how you feel."

My eyes widen at her words.

"You'll never move on if you don't, and you'll always regret it if you don't." She steps closer, placing her hand on my forearm. "You never know. If she's really 'sort of married' as you stated, she may be ready to move on. Maybe she has feelings for you, too. You never know."

I nod once, turn on my heel, and head to my room.

Lewis

Why did I do that? Why did I prompt her to ask me questions? I'm an idiot. The FBI has nothing on her interrogation techniques. She's relentless. I may have allowed her ten questions, but all I did was further stir her curiosity. And in turn, her advice left a gaping slice in my chest.

I'm bleeding. My heart struggles to pump as pain weighs me down. I erroneously thought talking about it might help settle my soul. Instead, it doubled—no, tripled—my heartache.

I needed to return to help Carter's family in his absence. I didn't plan for my lust to grow exponentially upon my return. I planned to keep myself busy with Ian and Ryan. I thought that by immersing myself in helping them, I'd have no time to fantasize. *Will this torture ever end?*

I climb into bed, already knowing I'm not falling asleep for hours, and when I do, I'm sure to see her in my dreams. It's the only place I allow myself to let loose and not hold back. In my dreams, I tell her how I feel as well as show her my love. My aching heart heals, and my soul's complete in my subconscious slumber. When I wake, these fantasies crack my chest open wider. They're a bittersweet visitor.

17

LEWIS

Later That Week

I lay a sleeping Ian in the crib for his nap then follow Ryan's voice to the kitchen. She leans her hips against the kitchen island, her back to me, phone in hand at her ear.

"No. Still the same," she answers into the receiver. "We'll continue with the same treatments, hoping for a miracle."

I sense the oppressive fear in her voice even though she's trying to sound positive to the caller.

"I will, Linda. Now, go play cards, and I'll talk to you next week." Ryan pauses to listen. "I will, and I love you, too. Bye."

I'm stunned silent, staring when Ryan turns around, placing her cell phone on the island.

"Hey," she greets.

"Mom?" I ask, unable to form a full sentence.

Ryan nods. "It's a good day. She knew who I was and asked about Ian."

My forefinger rubs my forehead as if rubbing out a crease there. "She has good days?"

Again, Ryan nods. "Not always on the day I call, but the nurses claim at least one good day per week."

"Can I...?"

"Next time I talk to her, you want to talk, too?" she asks, encouraging me.

"Yes," I answer, then quickly add, "if it's a good day."

"Okay," Ryan sweetly smiles. "A couple of the nurses have my number and text when Linda has a good morning, so I can call her then."

She shrugs as if this is nothing special. I'm sure Ryan's sweet demeanor and our family's tragic story prompted them to agree to text her. We've endured too much. *Heck, maybe that should be my next book.*

"She plays cards?" I manage to ask with a raspy voice.

"She plays pitch and bridge with other ladies, her friends," Ryan explains, eyes assessing me. "Even on bad days, she knows who they are and how to play. On her worst day, she thinks I'm a friend's daughter, calling to chat with her." She shrugs, pursing her lips. "I figure any conversation with her is special."

I nod. "Thank you."

Ryan's brow furrows. "For what?"

"For helping Carter find a home for her while I was overseas," I explain. "And for keeping in touch with her. I can't bring myself to ever make the call out of fear she won't know who I am."

Ryan nods, her hand reaching out to pat my forearm. She still amazes me with her fortitude. I'm here to help her, to support her, and she's somehow helping me. I've missed too much.

"So, tell me about the book you're writing," Ryan prompts during dinner when I emerge from the office over the garage.

"Well," I draw out, "it's the story Carter and I began plotting back in high school. We worked on it for one winter while we were snowed in, but busy with school, sports, and work, we lost interest in it after a few weeks."

She pauses, her fork midway to her mouth, smiling in hopes I continue.

"It's a coming-of-age tale in which the Ugly Duckling meets Jack and the Beanstalk," I brag.

Mouth full, her eyes blink as she processes my explanation. "Ah. Got it," she mumbles through her food, nodding.

I love that she supports my desire to write, allows me time and space to work, and encourages me to share my progress each day.

Mouth empty, she sips from her water glass before speaking again. "I'll start putting out some feelers among my author and editor colleagues.

When you're ready, we'll have plenty of places to send a query letter and manuscript to."

"I'm a long way from that step," I remind her.

"It never hurts to start the process and be ready when the time comes," she states, loading more steak on her fork and dipping it through the puddle of garlic butter on her plate. "Our firm works with several young adult authors, so I shouldn't have a problem getting you all set up."

"Thank you," I say between bites. "I've got a long way to go. I'm not even halfway through my first draft," I chuckle.

"I'd love to read chapters as you finish them," she informs me.

My stomach turns at the thought of sharing my writing with her. She's my favorite person. *Why am I afraid?* She handles promotions and editing with writers in her job. I should be no different. I think my writing at the present time is personal—very personal. It's in its infancy, not ready for critique or discussion. This will need to change through my writing process; it's vital that I share my work, listen to input, and improve upon my writing. Having never written outside of my college composition class and term papers, this is out of my comfort zone but a challenge I'm excited to accept.

"Hold still," I order, pulling out my cell phone, needing to get a photo of her in this light. She's gorgeous with the sunlight shining on her through the window above the sink as she rinses the supper dishes.

"Don't," she whines.

"Humor me," I plead, snapping photo after photo of her.

Lowering my phone, I scroll through to find the perfect shot to show her. She dries her hands on a nearby dish towel then takes my phone from my extended hand.

"Not bad," she comments, a large smile upon her face.

"Not bad?" I scoff. "You're gorgeous."

Her cheeks pink with embarrassment. She shakes her head in an attempt to shake off my words. I'll have none of it; she's beautiful, and she should know it.

18

RYAN

Days Later

I marvel at the sight of Lewis holding Ian to his chest in the nearby recliner. He's winey with a tummy ache but not feverish.

Suddenly, Ian coughs then pukes on Lewis's chest. Instead of laying my son down or gagging at the smell, Lewis places Ian on his outstretched thighs, and deftly removes his grey t-shirt. He wads it up and tosses it toward the laundry room then cuddles Ian tightly to his bare chest.

And oh, what a chest it is. *When does he find the time?* The guy must work out daily. There's not an ounce of fat anywhere. His biceps meld into sculpted shoulders and defined pectorals then flow to bump after bump over his abdominals. He doesn't have the heavy, bulging, drink-pre-and-post-workout-shakes type of muscles. He's got trim, lean, tight muscles. He's strong and sexy at the same time. *Damn. Life's not fair.* I could work out for hours daily and never achieve his results.

My husband was nothing to sneeze at. As identical twins, they've always been the same. His chiseled body was the product of laborious construction work every day. He carried a bit of extra weight around his waist due to his affection for beer and carbs. It wasn't a spare tire, but it certainly wasn't the sculpted vision currently taking up residence in my recliner.

STOP! This is so wrong.
He's my brother-in-law. I can't admire him.
Ew! Gross! What is wrong with me?

I know what's wrong with me. It's been 13 months since my husband passed away, I promote and edit romance novels for a living, and I will remain lonely for years to come.

"Ryan, are you okay?" Lewis smirks at my obvious ogling of him.

"You lied to me," I blurt. It's the only thing I could come up with to excuse my blatant staring.

"No, I didn't," he counters, still smirking, only now, his mouth quirks up on one side.

"You did not get that body from working long hours and sleeping in Dubai like you claim," I challenge.

"I didn't lie," he argues. "I stated I worked long hours in order to finish my contract ahead of schedule." He raises his free hand to prevent my next argument. "I said I rarely went anywhere but work and home. That's the truth. I used fitness equipment and free weights in my apartment. The laws in Dubai are strange by American standards. I opted to stay in so as not to wear the wrong thing, look at a woman the wrong way, or make a comment that landed me in a foreign jail."

"But those..." I point to his rippled abdominal muscles. "Those took hours."

He scoffs. He *actually* scoffs at me. "Working out helped me destress and wind down each night. You like what you see?" he teases.

"Just shocked," I retort. "I'm used to the string bean I roomed with in college."

"B.S!" he challenges then makes sure he didn't disturb Ian resting on his shoulder. "I was never a string bean, and you know it."

"That's how I remember it," I teasingly lie.

He often walked around our apartment senior year sans shirt. He worked out but was never this fine.

"Now, you're just..." He looks down at Ian and covers his ears. "...pissing me off. I worked out in college, and you know it."

"Fine. You may not have been a string bean in college, but you weren't..." I can't find words that don't sound sleazy.

"So, you *do* like what you see?" He grins knowingly.

Needing an escape from this conversation, I offer, "I'm running to the store. Do you need anything?"

His smirk turns into his sexy grin, the sexy smile that melted the hearts of all of the girls in college. *All but me, that is. Or did it?* I fell in love and married the mirror image of him.

19

RYAN

The Next Month

I'm sitting in the fertility doctor's exam room for the third time. Each visit reminds me of Carter and me attending obstetrics appointments during Ian's pregnancy. As if living with his mirror image isn't hard enough, I fear each visit and month of this hopeful pregnancy will call to mind more and more memories. Internally, I struggle with the positive outcomes a baby might bring to Ian warring with the sad memories of the husband I lost.

"Ahh, Ryan," the doctor greets upon entering the room, his nurse on his heels. "Has it been four weeks already?" His confident smile signals he knows full well it has been a month. He taps his stylus on his tablet, then his wide eyes and wide smile greet me. "Congratulations."

It seems odd to congratulate me on one full process of in-vitro. From what I've read, it's a long journey. Therefore, congrats every month is not necessary. I simply nod.

"If only all of my patients could be this successful in their quest for a baby," he continues, placing his tablet down and rolling his seat next to me.

Um, excuse me. What? Baby? You mean I'm...I'm frozen. It worked. It really worked. I'm pregnant. Holy cow.

"Ryan," the doctor calls. "Do you understand?"

"I'm sorry." I scramble to pull myself together. "I didn't... I mean... We hoped but didn't think we'd be pregnant after the first round."

He nods, his smile wider. "Given how easily you became pregnant with your first child and the fact you had been off birth control pills for several months, you were successful. That's a good thing, right?"

"Yes," I quickly reply. "We prepared for it to take months. That's all."

The nurse passes me informational pamphlets. The rest of the visit is a blur. I nod, take the referral to my OB/Gyn, and am sent on my way with many more congratulations from the staff.

Pulling into the driveway, I'm suddenly aware that I don't remember the drive home. I can't be that reckless; I'm all that Ian has left. Well, Uncle Lewis and I are all he has. I can't drive distracted. I need to make better decisions.

I grab my purse, lock my car, and enter the kitchen through the back door. I tilt my head to the side, attempting to hear where Ian might be. Nothing. I pull out my phone to text Lewis.

Me: Where are you?
Lewis: Office
Me: With Ian?
Lewis: Of course
Me: I'm home
Lewis: On our way

From the doorway, I watch the boys emerge from the office above the garage. Lewis points to me then waves; Ian waves, too. I smile widely as he seems to enjoy time with his uncle.

"So...?" Lewis prompts, stepping into the kitchen. "We set to repeat the process this month?" His eyes anxiously await my update.

"Uh-huh," I answer.

After a moment of silence, Lewis urges, "Um..."

He places Ian on the kitchen floor. My son crawls toward the toys in the front room. I pull water bottles from the fridge, extending one to Lewis.

"We can't try again this month," I announce, frantically searching for words.

The concerned look on his face causes me to hurry and explain.

"I'm..." I start. "We're," I point between the two of us with my index finger, "pregnant."

He drops his unopened water bottle, and I watch it roll under the edge of the counter.

"We're pregnant?" he asks, his voice raised several octaves.

"Yep." I smile.

A little scream escapes when I'm suddenly wrapped in a tight hug and lifted off the floor.

"Can't. Breathe," I croak.

"Oh, no." Lewis quickly returns me to the floor, his hands held out towards my belly. "Did I hurt you or..."

"No," I giggle. "The baby's protected right now."

I struggle to stop giggling at Lewis's reaction. Although I've experienced this before, he hasn't. I need to try and remember he's inexperienced and scared for the next nine months.

Lewis's teeth bite his lip as he proudly stares at my belly.

―――

The Next Morning

Damn pregnancy hormones.

It's happening again, this time without Carter. Heaven help me. I'm a widow, pregnant with my brother-in-law's baby, a single mom, and I'm horny twenty-four-seven.

Hmm. Do I still have toys? I used to keep them in my nightstand. Perhaps they are still there. *I mean, I haven't used them since before...*

Wow! Holy cow! Even thinking of losing Carter isn't enough to quell this feeling. *This is so screwed up.*

I need to remedy this situation—my situation. I learned while pregnant with Ian that the hormones continue to snowball all day long if I don't take care of it.

I walk from the kitchen into my bedroom, making a beeline for the drawer of my nightstand. My hand pauses midair as I contemplate which one before I jog to the bathroom.

As I lock the door, I mentally calculate that I have about five minutes that I may safely leave Ian playing in his portable crib in the living room while Lewis works in the office over the garage. It's almost lunch, and he takes his writing break at the same time on the days he works.

Moments later, as my body and thoughts float back to Earth, I mentally note to add batteries to my grocery list.

20

RYAN

Two Weeks Later

After weeks of waiting, today, we finally attend our first obstetrics appointment. Sensing my hesitation about Ian coming with us, as we prepare to walk into the office building, Lewis pauses, his hand on the door.

"He's healthy," he assures me. "And sick people go to general practitioners, not to see Obi Wan Kenobi."

I can't help but laugh, so hard, in fact, I snort. While laughing, I look at him through squinted eyes, trying to assess if he said that on purpose or if he really doesn't know what to call the doctor.

"Are you done?" he asks, acting affronted.

I nod, pressing my lips tightly together. Lewis holds Ian in one arm, opening the door for me with the other.

"Behave," I whisper in passing, not wanting him to embarrass me.

"What?" he asks, pretending to not know what I mean.

Near the still closed exam room door, Lewis stands frozen. I allow him several silent moments while I play pat-a-cake with Ian in my lap.

Eventually his eyes find mine. They're full of unshed tears. I extend my arm, placing my hand on top of one of his. His mouth opens and a gargled noise escapes.

He clears his throat before speaking again. "It's…We're pregnant."

I lick my lips before allowing a sly smile to climb upon my face. It feels good to have something worth smiling about. I nod.

"You're having my baby," he states, pulling Ian and me tightly to his chest.

With my ear pressed firmly against him, I feel his laughter vibrate in his chest while he hugs us. He smells of soap with a slight hint of musk. I close my eyes, drawing in a long pull of his scent through my nose. Along with his hard chest and warm embrace, it's heady. I allow myself this moment, just a minute to be safe and happy in his embrace.

When his lips place a peck upon the top of my head, every muscle tightens. Feeling my reaction, he releases me, keeping his hands upon my shoulders. He bends slightly to bring himself to my eye level, his blue eyes searching mine.

"This is what we wanted, right?" he inquires.

I nod and lose my battle at holding back my tears. My right hand covers my mouth as my sinuses burn and tears flow down my cheeks.

"I'm happy," I vow, despite my body language.

It doesn't look like he believes me. His hands don't leave my shoulders as his eyes turn softer.

"I'm happy. It's just…" I fan my overheated face. "I know we talked about it… Now, it's real."

"And real's a good thing, right?" He seeks more proof, lifting Ian from my lap.

"It's the hormones," I lie. I can't tell him how good it felt in his arms or how good he smells. I can't ask him to hold me tightly and never let me go, and I can't share how scared I am that carrying my best friend and brother-in-law's baby might ruin our relationship. It's the only relationship in my life right now that doesn't involve a diaper.

He pulls me closer, wrapping his arms around me once again, just not as tightly this time. I swear he sniffs my hair before moving his mouth toward my ear.

"It's going to work," he promises. "We'll make it through the pregnancy. I'll try not to become overprotective or annoy you, and when our baby arrives, Ian will get the bone marrow transplant he needs so the four of us can live long, happy lives together."

"It's that easy?" I challenge, voice barely above a whisper.
"I hope so," he chuckles, squeezing me.
"Me, too," I murmur. "Me, too."

21

RYAN

Back at The Car

"That was anticlimactic," Lewis states half-an-hour later, buckling Ian into his car seat.

I wait until he climbs in the driver's seat to respond. "The first couple of months are a fuzzy sonogram, labs, and answering questions," I inform him. "It's all in the pregnancy book I loaned you." I look pointedly toward him, reminding him he needs to read it. "I'll start to show soon if this pregnancy is like Ian's. You'll find things are much more exciting from four months on."

"Well, I intended for the office visit to be exciting and continue with a surprise for you," he states, keeping his eyes on the road.

Staring at his profile, I admire the crinkled corners of his mouth as he grins, his strong jawline, and his perfectly proportioned nose. He really is too attractive to remain single.

"You should start dating," I tell him, returning my eyes to the road in front of us, curious where he's taking us.

"Where'd that come from?" he chuckles.

"You left the country to get over a married woman. Now, you're back, so you should put yourself out there again," I explain.

"I'd rather focus on Ian and you," he states.

Does he think that is a reason not to date?
"You can help us and still date," I scoff.
"Maybe I don't want to," he retorts.
What does he mean he doesn't 'want to'? Surely, he isn't happy, still hung up on the married mystery woman. If only I had friends, I'd be able to set him up on blind dates. I'll just keep mentioning it; maybe he'll reconsider.
"Put this over your eyes," he orders, changing the subject.
"What? No way," I argue as he waves a blindfold in my direction.
"I have a surprise. So, hurry up, or you'll ruin it," he urges.
I roll my eyes and shake my head. *I can't believe I am doing this.* I pull the eye mask over my head and adjust it to conceal everything.
"I'll get car sick," I warn.
"We're pulling up now," he states.
At his words, I wish I'd paid attention during the drive. I don't know if we are on a busy street or what businesses we are near.
When he parks, turning off the car, I unfasten my seatbelt then cross my arms over my chest. If he wants me to get out, he's going to have to help me.
I listen intently as he lifts Ian from his car seat then walks to the passenger door. I turn my head in his direction as the door opens.
"Give me your hand," his deep voice orders, and I comply.
"Now, swing toward me," he instructs, his hand in mine. "Be careful of the curb."
I don't like moving in an unknown area without using my eyes. I begin to panic when he releases my hand until I feel him tight at my side, his palm placed firmly on the small of my back.
"It's flat here," he informs. "Nothing to worry about."
Right. Nothing to worry about. Is he aware of every crack or shift in the concrete? Is he watching for low tree limbs or birds flying in my direction? Clearly, I have trust issues. That thought causes me to chuckle.
"You okay over there?" he teases.
"Peachy keen," I tease back.
"Okay. Stop right here," he demands, removing his body from beside mine.
As much as I didn't trust him before, I now begin to freak out in his absence. I swing my arms wide in all directions, attempting to feel my surroundings.
"You can take the blindfold off now," he laughs.
I push the black sleep mask over my forehead. Both hands fly to cover

my eyes from the much-too-bright afternoon sunlight. I blink rapidly, trying to adjust as my eyes water a bit.

"Where are we?" I ask, taking in the driveway we stand in and the neighborhood around us.

Lewis points at the house in front of us. "What do you think?"

I look at him, trying to decipher what he's asking me. He lifts his chin towards the large stone-front ranch. I squint, assessing the home. It's large, with light gray stone and a colonial-blue front door. I turn to face Lewis and my son.

"It's ours," he boasts.

It's ours. It's ours? He can't be serious. He is serious. Oh. My. Gosh. He did it. He really did it. He bought this house.

"You didn't," I hedge, turning back to inspect the house.

"I did. It's ours." His crooked grin and twinkling eyes say it all.

"Wh… Ho…" I stutter, unable to process this news.

"Breathe in as you count to three," he urges. "Breathe out as you count to three."

I follow his instructions, repeating them another time.

"Shall we look at the inside?" he offers, signaling for me to lead the way to the front door.

I scan the yard and don't see a realtor.

"You have a key?" I ask.

"Yes," he chuckles. "I told you it's ours." He pulls a keyring from his front shorts pocket, dangling it in front of my face. "Follow us."

With Ian looking at me over his shoulder, Lewis unlocks the door and motions for me to enter in front of them.

Holy crap! My entire house could fit in this open kitchen, living room, and dining room area.

"It's huge," I blurt.

"That's what she said," Lewis quips.

I shake my head; I set him up good for that one. I know better in his presence.

"This is… Wow!"

"There's plenty of room for the four of us," he boasts. "Go check out the master."

I walk in the direction he points, stepping through the open doorway; it's humongous. Large windows line one wall with a view of the backyard. I peek around a corner into a giant, walk-in closet facing a large master bathroom. I run my fingers along the granite countertop between the his-and-her sinks with a large mirror hanging above each. I marvel at the glass-enclosed tile shower stall and the huge whirlpool tub. I spin slowly, admiring the beautiful space. Facing the doorway, I spy Lewis, smiling proudly at me with Ian's head resting on his shoulder.

"Wow!"

"You haven't seen it all," he states. "Let's go look at the other bedrooms."

The other bedrooms he speaks of are two rooms with a Jack-and-Jill bathroom between them on the opposite end of the house. Tears well in my eyes. They're perfect for Ian and our new baby. *Wait.* One would be Lewis's room and the other for the kids. I reassess the bedrooms, finding them too small for an adult man.

"Now, follow me downstairs," he orders, exiting before me.

I follow him into the open space then down the stairs. With no door above the steps, I'll need a baby gate to keep Ian from falling down them. I drag my hand down the railing as the stairs open into a large family or game room, complete with a full bar, pool table, and a gas fireplace.

"I thought this might be my room," he shares.

"It's a perfect man cave," I agree.

"Um, I meant this room." He stands in front of a closed door to one side of the large game room.

When he opens the door, I slip inside. It's a second master suite. *Oh, this is perfect.* It's much bigger than the guest room he currently sleeps in, and he'll have a private bathroom. I'm falling in love with his new house.

"There's one more room to see," he states, ushering me through the next door mere feet from his bedroom door. "I thought I'd finish this space, turning it into our offices."

We stand in a concrete room as large as a bedroom. Beams line the ceiling while both the walls and floors are exposed concrete. It will take more work than the area above my garage did. I arch an eyebrow in his direction.

"Trust me," he smirks. "I can handle it."

Smiling, I nod.

"So, what do you think?" he asks.

"It's perfect." I grin, shrugging.

"Wait until you see the backyard. Ian's going to love it," he states, swinging an arm for me to take the stairs.

I already marvel at his house, and I haven't seen the backyard or garage yet. I still love the little house Carter and I purchased to begin our family in.

Lewis opens the French doors off the kitchen, and I step onto a large, stone patio. *Wow!*

"The privacy fence with a locking gate is perfect. There's lots of room for Ian to run and play," he brags. "I thought I could install a swing and a playhouse over there. It would be in full view of the patio and from the kitchen."

He's right. I can't imagine allowing Ian to play when I'm not within a few feet, but he's right. It's a perfect play area for kids.

"Lewis, it's perfect."

"So, you like it?" he asks, needing to make sure.

"I love it."

22

RYAN

That Evening

"We need to talk," I state, when I return to the kitchen after putting Ian to bed.

Lewis continues loading the dishwasher.

"I love your house, but Ian and I can't live there with you."

His hands freeze with a plate above the dishwasher rack. He tilts his head and furrows his brow.

"I can't ask you to live with us forever." I raise my palm toward him when he starts to interrupt me. "You deserve love; you deserve a family. Living with us, you won't put yourself out there, and that's not fair. You need to date, and I won't cramp your style."

"Let me worry about that," he argues, setting the plate on the counter and stepping toward me. "I bought the house for the four of us. I want to live together as a family. Neither of us know what the future will bring. For now, I want us to focus on Ian and the baby."

He doesn't let me argue and places two fingers to my lips. His liquid eyes hypnotize me, paralyze me. He wraps his arms around me, pulling me to his chest. I allow him to surround me with his warmth, his strength, and his manly scent. I feel his words rumble in his chest.

"I bought the house for all of us," he states again. "I'm where I want to be. Ian and you need help, and I want to be with you."

I stare at the moon peeking through my bedroom window, the excitement of my day refusing to allow me to sleep. Last I checked, it was 1 a.m. I won't look at the time again as it doesn't help.

He bought a house. A house. Lewis shopped online and bought a house for all of us. It's perfect. *Of course, it's perfect. Everything Lewis does is perfect.* From the garage to the square footage to the yard and even the storage, it's absolutely perfect. Of course, he argues that it needs an office and a playground in the backyard, but those aren't necessities, at least not right now. I love Lewis's excitement to attend the obstetrics appointment with me and to surprise me with the house. My mind, however, focuses on his words from this evening.

"I want to be with you." My mind struggles to process his meaning. "I'm where I want to be. Ian and you need help, and I want to be with you." I'm grateful for his assistance and company the past couple of months. I'd be lost without him. "I want to be with you." *Is "you" plural or singular? Does he want to be with Ian, the baby, and me or with me?*

For hours, I relive every conversation and touch. In recent weeks, his touches have grown more frequent. I'm sure I'm overthinking it all; his touches have been innocent. *He's my best friend. Best friends hug and hold each other when they cry. But do they place chaste kisses on temples and the crown of the head? They were innocent kisses; they have to be. He's my best friend and brother-in-law, he's Ian's uncle, and he's the father to my unborn child. He's Lewis. That's all.*

23

RYAN

One Month Later

I don't want to go. I need to reschedule. With Ian in the hospital, I should be at his bedside, not going to my second-month obstetrics appointment. It'll just be labs, nothing important, so I could reschedule.

Lewis all but forced me from Ian's room as I fought tears, though. He's excited for this pregnancy. I've been there and done it already. I know what to expect, thus I don't want to do this. I worry Lewis will call the doctor's office to check on me, so I must go through the motions.

To my surprise, when I check in, I don't get to sit in the waiting room. I'm swept through the door to the scales. I pee in the cup, follow the nurse to the exam room, and I answer all the normal questions. Before she exits, the door opens, and my doctor walks through.

"Well, looky here. It's my favorite patient." He smiles.

"I bet you say that to all of the women," I retort, causing him to chuckle.

"How about we take a look with a sonogram today?" he offers.

I'm stone-still as fear washes over me. I didn't know there would be a sonogram. Lewis should be here. I can't believe he's going to miss this.

"Ryan, are you okay?" the nurse asks, her hands frozen above my exposed abdomen with the gel.

I nod, realizing I feel tears on my cheeks.

"Ian's back in the hospital, and Lewis will miss the first sonogram," I weep.

My doctor stands at my side, hand on my shoulder. "I want to keep a close eye on your pregnancy," he explains. "I understand you are under a lot of pressure with Ian's illness, so I'd like to do a sonogram today."

I wipe my tears with the tissue the nurse hands me. "It'll be fine. He will be disappointed. That's all."

"I'd rather not wait until next month," my doctor explains.

I let out a loud puff of air. "Let's do this."

Wasting no time, he places the wand over my lower abdomen, spinning it this way and that while I watch the fuzzy monitor. It's a sea of white and black. How they learn to read these is beyond me.

"Here we go," he cheers, freezing the wand in place to take a screenshot. He measures the baby and states it's on target. "Hold on…"

My breath catches. *No. No. NO! Please no!*

"Lookie here." He points with his free hand to another blob on the screen. "It's twins."

Twins? Twins!

"Healthy?" I ask, needing to calm my fear.

"All seems as it should be," he responds. "Let me see… I want to look from over here… There!"

He snaps a screenshot then hands the wand to the nurse before turning to me.

Standing by the monitor, he points. "This is baby one, and here is baby two." He makes an oval around them. "This is one sac and one placenta." He looks from the screen to me. "Identical twins."

Identical twins. I take a moment to process this. It shouldn't be a surprise. Carter and Lewis were identical; it runs in the family.

Returning from my thoughts, I see the doctor offering sonogram print-outs to me.

"These are my first identical twins," he brags.

"Lewis and Carter were identical," I remind him, having told him during my first appointment.

He nods. "We'll keep a good eye on the three of you every step of the way. There will be differences between your first pregnancy and this one. I'll get some handouts for you, and there are great prenatal books on the subject of twins."

I nod, a bundle of nerves. Now, I have two big news items to share with Lewis. He'll be doubly disappointed that he missed today's appointment.

We wrap up the appointment, and I make my way back to Ian's hospital room. My hands shake as I push open the door.

"Hey, you," Lewis greets, rising from his chair to step towards me. I note Ian sleeping nearby. "What'd the doctor say?"

Lewis stands in front of me, much like a child, excited for news. I slide the two sonogram photos from my purse, offering them to him.

He looks from my hand to my face and back.

"I'm sorry. I didn't know. They don't usually do sonograms this early in a pregnancy," I explain.

He shakes his head. "It's okay." His hoarse voice expresses his emotions clearly. "Tell me what I am looking at here." He spins the photos this way and that, hoping to decipher them.

I point to one kidney-bean shape. "This is the baby," I inform. I move my finger before continuing. "This is the other baby."

I bite my lips, hiding my smile at his scrunched brow and pursed lips as he tries to see what I've shown him.

"This blob is a baby?" he asks, pointing to the first spot I showed him.

I'm sure he thought it would look like a tiny human.

"And this blob is the other baby," I repeat.

This time, it registers. His eyes fly to mine, and I nod.

"Two?" He holds up two fingers between us.

"Yes."

"Twins..." His voice is full of wonder.

"Identical twins," I clarify.

He squints, pulling the photo up close. "Boys or girls?"

"I didn't ask as I don't want to know. If we find out, I want to wait until the four to five month mark like a normal pregnancy."

"I wanted to find out from the DNA at the in-vitro clinic," he reminds me. "This is definitely not a *normal* pregnancy, so we should find out."

I shake my head. "Nice try," I chuckle. "I feel stupid that I didn't consider twins as a possibility."

"Well, it skips a generation in our family," he informs me. "Or until now, it's been every other generation."

"Lucky us," I fake cheer.

"Superhuman sperm," he claims.

I shake my head at my hilarious friend, fighting a huge smile.

24

LEWIS

Weeks Later

Safely at home, Ian giggles at the block tower as it tumbles to the carpet. He enjoys handing Ryan and me blocks to construct a tower then watching me knock it over. I'd do it a million times in a row just to hear his little boy giggles. Ryan excuses herself to find her cell phone as it signals a text from across the room. Ian doesn't watch her; his eyes stay on the blocks and me.

I'm building another, higher tower as Ryan makes a call. She leans on the arm to the recliner, not really sitting and not quite standing. Her face pales while she waits for the call to connect. I distract Ian with his plastic cow that moos when he moves it, rising from the floor.

"This is Ryan. You asked me to call." She speaks quickly.

She's silent for a moment before her eyes swing up to me. I watch in horror as they fill with tears.

No. No! No! Not now, not like this. I've focused on Ian and Ryan; I planned to fly to see Mom soon. *Not soon enough. Damn it!* This is the last thing Ryan needs. Another loss. Another heartache. I can't make this better. I can't shield her from this.

"I'm sorry," Ryan whispers, her mouth near my ear.

Only now do I realize her arms embrace me. She's comforting me. She's comforting me when I should be comforting her.

Slowly, my hands slide around her sides to her lower back. My arms squeeze her gently as I will my love to ease her pain, my body to give her security, and warmth to envelop her.

"I'm sorry you made that call..." I start to apologize.

"You have nothing to be sorry for," she claims, raising her head, her eyes finding mine. "She's in a better place."

I nod, understanding. Mom no longer feels the frustration of knowing but not knowing at the same time.

"She's with Dad and Carter," I whisper.

A fire rises in my stomach, shoots up my spine, and explodes in my head. Suddenly, there's no air, no oxygen in the room. Like a guppy out of water, I fight for breath. A scream pierces the space.

"You're okay. I've got you," Ryan soothes as her hands slide up and down my back.

The scream. It's mine. My legs give out; my knees fall to the carpet, my head cradled in her hands at her abdomen. I don't fight the tears or the sobs.

"Let it out," she whispers, holding my head tightly to her stomach. "I've got you."

25

RYAN

Days Later

I remove my right hand from the laptop, my fingers playing with the short, thin, blonde hair on Ian's head. He sleeps soundly in my lap as I type my email to Lewis. I allow myself this distraction, this precious moment, praying I'll have many more years with my son. It may be wrong, but I find myself hoping Ian will live a life long enough that, like Lewis does now, he'll mourn my loss. I don't want this to end with me mourning his.

Lewis organized Linda's affairs at the time Carter and I moved her into the Alzheimer's Care Center, while he worked overseas. I have a copy of the documents somewhere. Tears fill my eyes, blurring my view of Ian. I didn't know, when Lewis left for Dubai, that Carter would die before we saw him again. I didn't know Ian would be diagnosed with leukemia after the loss of my husband while my best friend was halfway around the world. And Lewis couldn't have predicted Linda would pass before he planned to visit upon his return. He busied himself with Ian and me; it's our fault he didn't travel to Florida right away. He wasn't here when Carter died, and he wasn't there when his mother died. Now, I fear his guilt might eat him alive.

Upon his arrival in Florida, he found he must wait 48 hours after the cause of death is found before he may cremate his mother. Since Ian and I are the only family he has left and we can't travel, there will be no ceremony. Lewis will be present when her urn finds its eternal resting place beside her husband. While I understand he needs to be in Florida to see this through, I miss him already. I've come to find comfort with him nearby. Upon his departure, my anxiety rose as the horrible "what ifs" filled my thoughts. I refuse to take anxiety meds during my pregnancy; I won't do anything that might jeopardize Ian's chances at a healthy sibling match. Lewis will be home in a few days. I can cuddle my boy, urging his touch to calm me until then.

I rest my palm on Ian's cheek for a moment then upon my baby bump. I take several deep breaths, willing myself to believe Lewis will make it safely back to us. I pray he returns to us as I need him more with each passing day.

With Lewis's help and distractions, I no longer live each day waiting for the next shoe to drop. It's been over a month since I worried when the next bad thing would blindside me, and I have Lewis to thank for that. He's helping me find the joy in each day, in the little things, and to live in the moment. He keeps me grounded, on target, level-headed, and doesn't allow me to give up. He makes me smile, he makes me laugh, and he washes the pain away. I need to be strong until he returns.

It's a double-edged sword. While having him here as my best friend helps, he looks like Carter, which makes me miss my husband. I've longed to return to the time in my life when I had both by my side. However, to do that would mean Ian wasn't yet in my life. As difficult as it is with the doctor visits and hospital stays, I would never give up being Ian's mom. I must live with the knowledge that my little family rapidly deconstructed, but I'm constructing a new one bit by bit with each passing day.

26

LEWIS

Two Days Later

It's pouring down rain, and I'm dead-tired when I pull into the driveway. Five days away is too many. Noting no lights are on in the office above the garage, I jog to the house.

I leave my copies of the paperwork on the island in our kitchen. I'll file them in the office tomorrow. Right now, I need to see Ian, the babies' bump, and Ryan.

The house is quiet; I look at my phone. It's eight, which means Ian's in bed. I didn't expect the house to be quiet; maybe Ryan is working in her bedroom. As his room is closer, I slip into Ian's room first.

"Hey, little man," I whisper at the side of his crib. "I'm home. You sleep, and we will have our man-time tomorrow."

At the touch of my knuckles on his cheek, his little head turns to the other side, but he remains asleep. I kiss two of my fingers then softly press them to the top of his head. Next, I walk towards the master bedroom in search of Ryan.

I hear soft humming from the bathroom as I walk down the hallway. I move softly, hoping to sneak up on her as she hums to herself. Standing in the crack of the slightly opened bathroom door, I find Ryan soaking in a tub filled with bubbles, wearing earphones, eyes closed, humming to her music.

Her neck rests on a rolled-up towel, and her head is back, clearly relaxing. I don't want to disturb her. She's been on her own for several days, so she's probably tired. Looking around, I note she has her vanilla candles lit, and the lights remain on. I reach my hand around the corner, flipping off the light switch. With a washcloth resting over her closed eyes, she doesn't notice the drastic change in lighting. I decide to leave her alone a bit longer, walking to the kitchen for a beverage.

Ryan

When my warm bath fades to cooler temperatures, I remove the cloth from my eyes and lift my head. *Something's off.* I look around the tiny room for a clue of what is different. I shake my head. Nothing's changed.

I turn the dial to raise the plug with my foot. At the sound of water flowing down the drain, I stand, reaching for my Terry cloth robe. Sensing something I can't put my finger on, I scan the room once more. *Hmm...*

It's when I take a step towards the sink that I hear a noise from outside the bathroom. I tilt my head to the side, attempting to hear better. I hear nothing more, so I look toward my handheld video baby monitor. Ian rests safely in his crib. I shake it off. With Lewis away, I've heard many sounds this week. I bend at my waist, cupping water from the faucet to my face, rinsing off my moisturizing mask. Face clean, I blot it with a nearby hand towel.

I startle at the sound of a large clank. *That's not my imagination or the house settling.* I look around my bathroom for something to defend myself with. *Hairspray or plunger? Hairspray or plunger?* I opt for the hairspray then make my way into the hall, spray can cocked and ready.

I pause when I hear indistinct murmuring from the kitchen. *Is Lewis home?* It could be after eight; he could be home. Not taking any chances, I tiptoe toward the kitchen, hairspray in hand. Slowly, I take one step and then two.

"Lewis?" I call, my voice just above a whisper.

"Yeah," he answers from the kitchen.

"Thank goodness." I breathe a sigh of relief. "I thought you were a burglar."

He looks up from the pan on the floor to my face and then my hand.

"What were you going to do with that?" he asks, chuckling and pointing to the hairspray.

"It's all I could find in the bathroom," I defend. "I thought I could spray the jerk in the eyes and then find something else to use."

His chuckle morphs into a deep, masculine laugh.

I'm so happy he's home.

"Find a seat," he orders, pan now tucked into the cabinet. "I need to share some details."

He doesn't need to finish the statement; I know it's about Linda's passing.

"Within a week, you'll receive a check in the mail for Ian and you," he shares.

My face scrunches, unsure what he means. "I don't want a check," I state.

"Carter would have received a check if he were still here." I see the pain this statement causes him. He's exhausted. "In his absence, his share is split half in a trust for Ian and half in a check to you," he explains.

I shake my head.

"It's what my parents wanted," he defends.

I fight the tears welling in my eyes. I've lost too many people in just over a year and dealt with too many death benefits. It's exhausting.

"They worked hard for their money and invested it wisely," he informs me, even though I already know. "It was their goal in life to save money for their children and grandchildren. They were proud they succeeded. Please, make them happy and accept it."

"How much?" I shouldn't ask, but I need to be prepared.

"You'll need to meet with a financial planner," he begins, taking my hand in his. "I'll share my guy's contact with you."

I nod. "It's that much?"

"I thought Carter shared this information with you when you placed mom in the home." He tilts his head to the side.

"I never asked or looked through the binder," I confess. "It wasn't important to me."

"Well, it's important now." His lips attempt a slight smile. "It's seven figures."

Thousands, ten-thousands, hundred-thousands, then millions... I cough, unable to breathe. *What will I do with seven figures?*

27

RYAN

Two Weeks Later

I rotate my neck slowly from one side to the other; my neck muscles are tight from hours of computer work. I snag the page of notes, hoping they'll spark ideas for graphics as I lay in bed tonight. I notice the page contains more doodles than ideas. Several infinity symbols skirt the margins in varying shades of black ink.

Descending the steps from my office above the garage, I swing my arms in circles like a windmill, attempting to loosen my shoulders. I lost track of time as I worked to finish two more graphics for my authors. The sun already dips behind the trees; I'm sure Ian went to bed hours ago.

Quietly slipping through the kitchen door, I find the house lit only by a dim light from the television in the living room. I use the flashlight from my cell phone to help me safely maneuver through the stacks of moving boxes. I'm ready for the next two days to be over and to never see a moving box again.

"I'm home," I sing in a whisper, stepping into the front room, not wanting to wake Ian in his nearby room.

"Hell yeah," Lewis slurs from the floor, a beer in his hand.

My head tilts, unsure why he might be over imbibing tonight. Maybe it has something to do with our move in the next two days.

"Partying without you," he says, or at least that's what I think he says; it's hard to understand him. "Everything boxed until…"

I quirk my head, waiting for him to finish his statement. He doesn't.

"I'm going to warm up some leftovers," I inform him, turning back to the kitchen.

"Only have paper plates left," Lewis states, fumbling to stand.

I contemplate letting him do it himself but remember my sleeping son. If Lewis bumps into a stack of boxes, it's sure to make lots of noise.

"Here." I offer my extended hand. "On the count of three."

On three, I pull hard, and as he stands, I lose my balance. He catches me before I fall.

"Easy." His quick reflexes aren't those of an inebriated man. His right-hand splays on my stomach. "Can't have you hurting anyone."

My breath catches, my heart stops, and I'm sure my eyes bug out at his touch. I don't mind people touching my pregnant belly; it happened all too often with Ian. Lewis's hand so near his children, though… It's paternal, it's intimate, and I can feel his love for our little ones. My hand moves to cover his, and his ice-blue eyes turn liquid.

"Thanks. We're all okay," I promise in a whisper.

His eyes close for two seconds, and when they open, he seems to snap out of his previous thoughts. His hand slips from beneath mine, he twines our fingers together, and he leads me into the kitchen, flipping on the light as we go.

"I don't like you skipping meals," he shares, pulling a paper plate with two slices of pizza from the nearly empty fridge.

When he prepares to place them in the microwave, I speak up. "I like it cold."

He knows this; my dorm mini fridge frequently held cold pizza for me to enjoy anytime, day or night. It became his habit to order extra pizza to ensure I'd have leftovers.

He hands me the paper plate and a cold bottle of water then opens another beer for himself.

"Why the party?" I ask, lifting my chin at the beer.

"Figured it's easier to drink it than to move it tomorrow." He shrugs, smirking.

I love his smirk; it's devilish, boyish even. I love his sexy smile. I love everything about his expressive face.

"We've got a big day tomorrow," he states, watching me chew a bite of pepperoni pizza. "Why don't you finish that in bed?"

I nod, heading to my bedroom. Once I swallow, I bid him good night.

Later, I turn on the overhead light, already missing my bedside lamp that's tucked away in one of the hundred boxes scattered about. According to my cell phone, it's just after midnight; looks like I won't be sleeping again tonight. I experienced sleepless nights at the end of Ian's pregnancy, but never during the first two trimesters. I may be in for a long, uncomfortable pregnancy this time around.

"What's wrong?" Lewis murmurs from the doorway.

"I can't sleep," I state, not wanting to tell him what's swimming inside my mind tonight. "What are you doing up?"

"My room's all packed, so I'm crashing in the living room tonight. Want me to rub your back?" he offers through a yawn.

"Not sure that will help," I share honestly.

"Crawl back in. Let's try."

I scoot toward the head of the bed on my behind, my eyes on Lewis. Too late to turn down his offer, I realize he's shirtless and in fitness shorts. There's no way I'll be able to relax with a shirtless Lewis in his brother's bed, his brother's bedroom, on the last night in his brother's house. This will perpetuate the thoughts that drove me from my bed in the first place. I sit with my back against the headboard in the center of the bed.

Lewis takes one step inside the doorway, flipping the light off as he moves toward the bed. "I'll stay on top of the covers," he promises, climbing in beside me.

Our arms touch, but I don't scoot over. I'm not willing to sleep on the far side of the bed—Carter's side.

"Roll over," he orders, his hand pushing my shoulder to comply.

Slowly, I slide from the headboard, lay my head on a pillow with both of my hands clutching it tightly. Lewis's hand starts making small circles on the area between my shoulder blades. Through the soft cotton of my t-shirt, it feels divine.

"Relax," he urges. "Your back's tight."

"It's from working at my desk for so long today," I inform him. "My neck and shoulders are tight, too."

"You close your eyes, work on relaxing, and I'll work on getting the kinks out for you," he says, no longer slurring his words.

I pull in a long breath, count to three, then release it. Deep breaths in and out, in and out. His fingers feel heavenly on my back, my shoulders, and my neck, but even that doesn't distract me from the fact that this is my last night in the house Carter and I bought, in the bed we shared.

I hold my breath, and Lewis's hand stills as the rustling of Ian rolling over sounds through the baby monitor. At the sound of his little snore, I release my breath, and the rubbing commences. I enjoy his efforts for many long minutes.

"I miss this," I confess in a whisper, tears in my eyes.

"What?" he whispers back.

"Him," I share, wiping tears from my cheeks.

28

LEWIS

Later

"I miss this... Him."

Her words are a bucket of cold water on my thoughts of how nice it feels to hold Ryan in my arms. I can't be in here like this. I climb from the bed, immediately exiting her bedroom.

I lean against the hallway wall mere inches from her door. My heart is torn between the pain she feels without Carter and the feelings I've had for *her* from the first day of our business law class. My lungs burn; I can't seem to pull in enough oxygen.

I'm not an idiot. I know she loved my brother; she loved him with all of her heart. Hell, she still loves him. It's the reason I took the job in Dubai. I loved her, and she loved him.

Living with her, my love for her multiplies daily. While I was away, I missed her goofy little snort when she laughed hard, the way she pinched her nose before pulling laundry from a hamper...everything about her.

Her whispered confession through her tears was a punch in the gut. Not because she's thinking of and missing him, but because I don't want to rush her, and I never want to replace him. I'm at war with my own feelings on top of hers.

My breath catches at the sound of her continuing sobs. I want to climb back into bed with her, to hold her until her tears end, yet I can't. I'm not that strong anymore. Slowly, my body slides down the wall to sit.

After a half an hour of fighting my own tears while listening to hers, she finally drifts to sleep. I crawl on my hands and knees to the edge of her bed. I listen to her steady breaths and watch the slight rise and fall of her shoulders. My right hand reaches for her; I pull it back. *Not yet.* I can't show her all my cards tonight. I exit her room as I entered, on all fours. In the hall, I lie down just outside her door, my head on my arm. I feel I need to remain close in case she wakes.

"Lewis?" Ryan's raised voice startles me from slumber.

"Hey," I greet, struggling to sit up after my long night on the hardwood floor.

"What… Why are you sleeping in the hallway?" She implores.

"I wanted to listen for Ian and be near in case you woke up again," I confess, rubbing my stubbled jaw.

I pop my neck by turning it to the right and then the left. Sleeping on the hard floor wasn't the smartest choice. My body's going to make me pay for it all day.

Ryan shrugs, excusing herself for her morning coffee.

"Fix me a cup," I call after her.

She doesn't agree, doesn't stop to look back my way. She simply waves over one of her shoulders. *Is it me, or is she different this morning?* I mean, she's not a peppy morning person, but she's not a grouch either. We've got a busy day today; the movers arrive in an hour, followed by our five-month baby appointment and sonogram before lunch. I pray our interactions last night won't make today awkward.

29

RYAN

Later

I fix Lewis's cup of coffee first then prepare my decaffeinated cup. I haven't admitted it to him, but I love the new single cup coffee maker he bought for us. I think my comments about him switching to decaf to share a pot with me worried him. He insists this machine makes better coffee; I think he feels less guilty.

"Look who I found," Lewis says, walking into the kitchen carrying Ian. "He's got a fresh diaper and is ready for some breakfast. Aren't you, buddy?"

I turn to face the guys, two cups of coffee in hand. When Lewis reaches for his, I pull it away.

"Put him in his chair first," I suggest, carrying the coffee to the island. "What should we have for breakfast?" I ask, noting every cabinet I open is empty.

"Cereal's here." Lewis pulls two from an opened moving box. "I think there's enough milk left in the fridge for the two of us." He fetches the milk, placing it near our coffees. "I packed all of the bowls. Crap!" he curses, then thinks better of it and covers his mouth.

My eyes stare at my hands on the counter, and I try to stifle my laughter. We've discussed that Ian's of the age where he'll soon repeat anything we say, so we're trying to clean up our language. My giggles morph to laughter, and I snort, not once but twice.

"You're laughing now," Lewis murmurs, suddenly near my ear. "When he repeats the cuss words, you won't be laughing." His index finger lifts my chin, allowing our eyes to meet. "Your potty mouth is worse than mine," he professes, his finger bopping me on the tip of my nose.

His playfulness makes my awful mood more obvious. I'm tired. It's been several nights since I've slept longer than five hours. The pregnancy hormones have ramped up, causing my moods to fluctuate minute by minute, and I'm always horny. Combined with my excitement for the move and my hesitation to leave behind my memories of Carter with this house, I'm a mixed-up mess. I need to snap out of my funk; today is supposed to be exciting.

"Are we still doing it?" I ask, looking around for something that might work as a bowl.

"That's what she said," he retorts, handing me the one red plastic cup we have left.

I shake my head at his comeback and my innate ability to keep setting him up for it. I take his proffered cup, pour my favorite cereal in, then douse it with milk.

"Hmm," I mumble, scanning the kitchen. "Spoons?" I look to Lewis.

He mouths, "Crap," and begins reading the labels he placed on each moving box. I tap him on the shoulder, and when he turns, I demonstrate I can drink the cereal from the cup.

"Genius," he compliments, then pours dry cereal onto Ian's tray.

"My turn," he announces, lifting my glass to his mouth.

I roll my eyes. I secretly love the way he eats my food.

"Now, what were you asking earlier?" He reminds me of my question.

"I was asking if you still want to find out..."

"Yes!" he excitedly interrupts. "I mean, if you do."

I can't deny him. It's all he's talked about lately, and he's spent the entire pregnancy trying to persuade me to find out the sex of the babies. He followed my lead when I declined finding out the sex of the embryo during our in-vitro process. While he hounded me, I realized I don't mind finding out at the fifth month sonogram as is the norm. I wasn't ready in the beginning.

"As long as you promise not to paint and go hog wild buying stuff, I'm okay with finding out," I share. "It's not that I'm not excited about having the babies. I'm just worried we'll be told one thing and then have the other."

He nods, smiling the sexy smile that I love, then bites his lips between his teeth.

"What?" I ask.

"Prepare for all possibilities," he explains.

I nod; he's right. He knows me so well. I plan for all possible outcomes. I did it with Ian, and I'm doing it now.

"I think we're having boys," he informs me.

"Oh, you do, do ya?" I smile.

He wraps his arms around my waist and pulls my back to his chest, his hands on my belly with his mouth near my right ear. He murmurs, "Twin boys."

I turn in his arms, arching my back to look up, and state, "Twin girls; moms know these things." I really have no idea. I just love teasing him.

He leans his forehead to mine, eyes peering into mine. "I can't wait to meet them."

I close my eyes, biting my tongue. Part of me hopes it's boys if that is what Lewis wants, even if I really have my heart set on baby girls.

30

LEWIS

An Hour Later

I reach out to brush blades of grass off the base of Carter's headstone. There's something eerie about looking at the grave of an identical twin. In some ways, I feel I'm looking at my own grave. Our bond is closer than ordinary brothers, even from the grave.

"I never know how to begin our conversations nowadays," I confess, unshed tears clogging my throat and burning my sinuses. "It'd be so much easier if you'd speak to me." I chuckle at the thought of Carter haunting me as a ghost and shake my head.

"Honestly, your words from our heart-to-heart no longer haunt me; the loss of you spurred me into action." Again, I chuckle, but it's hollow. "I know what you'd say to me if you could. 'I wasted my chance. Remember, if you snooze, you lose.' And you are right."

"I must confess I spent many years being envious of you. I'm sure you knew it; I wasn't the best at hiding it. I just need you to know I'm snoozing no more. I'm finally doing what I needed to in the year before you met Ryan."

Silently sitting on my knees, I gaze at my brother's final resting place as I recall our plan that backfired and the repercussions of it. Carter took a long weekend off from his construction job to visit me at college my junior year.

He'd heard me wax on about a girl in my study group who turned into my best friend that I longed to ask out but hadn't found the right time. In the hour before we were set to meet my friends, including Ryan, at the college bar, we devised the plan. I'd introduce Carter to Ryan, he'd pull her aside, feed her flattering stories about me, then drop the hint that I wanted to ask her out but worried I'd lose her friendship.

Of course, our plan was flawed. Try as he might, Carter was unable to separate Ryan from the group. In a last-minute Hail Mary attempt, he asked her out, and she said yes. To this day, I'm still shocked she accepted his date request. Knowing Ryan as I did, she and Carter were opposites. He preferred the school of life to her scholarly pursuits. He lived life as it came where she planned, plotted, and strove to achieve her goals. Bile rises in my throat even today at the memory of her saying "yes" to Carter so many years ago.

The following 24 hours were the longest of my life as I tried to have faith Carter could persuade her to take a chance on me and for her not to fall for him. The heart-to-heart that followed the "date" tore me to shreds. "Lewis, I fought it; I fought it with everything I had. I like her. I mean *really* like her. She's funny, she's easy-going, she's… Man, I failed you."

I didn't doubt Carter's guilt over his feelings for Ryan then, and I still don't today. My brother loved Ryan with all he had. It killed me to watch Ryan fall for him, to listen to her talk about their dates, and to help my twin plan his proposal to the girl I loved. All the while, Carter saw my pain and jealousy; we talked about it. The night before he proposed, he offered to step aside to allow me to make my move. I couldn't deny Ryan her happily ever after, though. I couldn't ask Carter to sacrifice for me. I tried to look on the bright side, that Ryan would always be in my life, married to my brother; eventually, that was not enough.

I hid my feelings for her, remaining best friends. As her brother-in-law, we grew even closer, yet it still wasn't enough. My mind moves to another heart-to-heart with Carter.

"I'm taking the job in Dubai," I told him. "I've got to get away and clear my mind."

"Is it really so bad that you need to leave for four years?" he queried, concerned about my decision.

"I can't be here," I told him. "I've tried dating and one-night stands. Meaningless sex, no matter the quantity, hasn't erased my feelings. In fact, it didn't even distract me. I've got to leave everything, cleanse the system, and start anew; it's the only way I can move on."

"It's gonna upset her," Carter warned.

"It's gonna kill me," I reminded him.

The pain on her face when I told her about my job transfer will forever be burned in my memory. She tried to support me, to hide her pain, but she failed. The pain in my chest and the hurt in her eyes almost changed my mind.

I shift from my knees, placing my bottom on the green grass, my arms over my knees in front of me.

"I'm keeping my promise that I made at your funeral," I inform Carter what he must already know, watching me from heaven. "I plan to take care of Ian and Ryan forever. I'll never replace you, but I can be there for them."

I inhale a deep, cleansing breath, holding it for a moment before exhaling. "I love her. I've always loved her; you know that. I didn't think it was possible, but I love her more each and every day." I smile, shaking my head. "I fear I'm turning into the goofy, crazy-in-love man I used to tease you for being. I guess she does that to us. She's amazing."

I take another long breath. "I came here today to let you know I'm finally gonna make my move. You were right way back in college. There's never a perfect moment. So, I'm going to go ahead and make my move. Wish me luck." I rise to my feet, stepping closer to the granite. "I'll never replace you. I promise.

"Do what you can up there with the Big Guy to help Ian. I'd give anything for you to still be down here with the two of them." I release a long, slow breath. "Do me a favor and give me a sign from time to time to let me know you are with us every step of the way."

I clear the clog from my throat, tap my hand on top of the headstone, and return to my car.

I stop at the corner convenience store for the snacks I used as my excuse to get out of the house and hurry home to keep my promise to be there for Ryan when the movers arrive.

31

RYAN

At Home

I feel guilty that I'm not as outwardly excited as Lewis today. We're both exhausted from lack of sleep last night, and while mine shows, his faded. He scurried around after breakfast, packing up last minute items then ran to get us snacks for the day. He pulled into the driveway minutes before the moving truck arrived.

Beside me now, he sings along with the radio while driving us to our obstetrics appointment. His excitement at finding out the sex of the babies grows with each block we drive. I look at Ian over my shoulder. He's taking his morning nap in his car seat.

"I wish I were napping," I grumble from the passenger seat, jealous.

Lewis's right hand squeezes my knee. "You can nap on the air mattress at the new place while we wait for the movers to bring our stuff over."

An air mattress. That will be comfortable, I grumble to myself. Well, given my many nights of lacking sleep, it might just be comfortable enough. Lord knows I'll need my energy to begin unboxing this afternoon.

"We're here," Lewis announces, turning off the ignition. His anxious eyes glimmer with boyish charm. "I'll get Ian."

I slide from the bucket seat, vowing to be excited for Lewis. I reach for the diaper bag, but he beats me to it. His free hand in mine, we check in at the desk and sit in the waiting room while Ian sleeps on his shoulder.

Ten minutes later, back in the exam room, the nurse scurries to prep the sonogram as the doctor records my vitals and my answers to his questions.

"Ready?" my doctor asks, sonogram wand in hand.

I look up to Lewis as he smiles down at me. He squeezes my hand, and I nod to the doctor. We stare anxiously at the monitor while the doctor moves the device this way and that, recording measurements, tapping keys, and taking photos. Then, he focuses on one twin, turning back to us, an image frozen on the screen.

He doesn't need to tell me; I recognize it from Ian's sonogram. There's a tiny turtle shape. We're having boys.

"Ryan, you seem to already know," the doctor states, discerning my facial reaction.

I nod, looking up to Lewis. The confusion on his face turns to fear. I shake my head as I say, "Nothing's wrong. I promise. I can tell the sex from the screen." I quirk a smile.

Lewis looks from me to the screen to the doctor then back to me, eyes wide and seeking.

"Still want to know?" I ask him. At his nod, I reveal, "Boys."

"I knew it!" he shouts, startling Ian on his shoulder. He pats his back, soothing him to stay asleep. "We're having boys," he whisper shouts, a giant smile reaching the corners of his eyes, gracing his face.

I marvel at his reaction, his gloating, and the weight of our actions. In trying to save Ian, we've created identical twins. In a way, we've replicated his relationship with Carter. It's clear he's a proud father. And blast it all to hell, he was right, and I was wrong. I concede to the fact that I'll never have a daughter. There's no way I'm getting pregnant again. Three boys is enough.

"Better luck next time," Lewis offers teasingly.

I shake my head. "There won't be a next time."

I keep my eyes on the monitor as the doctor focuses on the second twin, confirming it's a male. I'm okay with my decision. Three boys, three *healthy* boys, will be enough for me.

Lewis

. . .

Boys. Twin boys like Carter and me. I'm truly blessed. Visions of football in the back yard and little league games flood my mind. Ian's healthy, and at only a year older, they will often play on the same teams. My three amigos will take the world by storm. My chest swells with pride. I never knew babies could have this effect on a grown man. Memories of Dad practicing with Carter and me play before me. I idolized my dad; I want to be that for my sons, for Ian and my boys.

I return to the present as Ryan tugs on my free hand. Looking around the exam room, I find we are alone. *Wow. When did that happen?*

"Ready to go?" she asks, smiling. "I can't believe he slept through your cheering."

I place a soft kiss on Ian's exposed cheek, my arm holding him tighter to my shoulder. He's the reason we're here; I can't forget that, no matter how excited I am to have Ryan carrying my sons.

"You're a dork," she giggles, tugging me to the car.

"Yes, but you're carrying this dork's babies," he retorts, tugging me back to his side. "I kind of zoned out back there."

"Ya think?" She scoffs. "Let me guess. Little league trophies and football games were all you could think about."

"Uh, no," I argue. "Dad and Carter were in some thoughts."

"You're so transparent," she chuckles, sliding into the passenger seat.

I close her door softly before placing Ian in his car seat. "They're my first," I remind her. "I get to be a little dad-crazy."

"Yes, you do." She grins, patting my forearm.

I take her hand in mine, lifting it to place a kiss on the back of it. I slowly raise my eyes to hers through my lashes. "You're amazing. You know that?"

Her smile widens and her eyes soften. "Don't you forget it," she teases.

"I won't," I vow.

Just you wait. I plan to show you just how amazing I think you are and so much more. I told Carter my plan this morning; now, it's time to show her how I feel.

Lewis

"Please," I beg Ryan, my hands on each of her shoulders. "Take Ian into the bedroom and nap on the air mattress. I'll take care of everything out here."

With the stubbornness I love, she opens her mouth to argue.

"The movers will start unloading in other rooms now since the master bedroom was the first to be loaded," I remind her. "I'll simply direct traffic and sort boxes that end up in the wrong rooms. There will be plenty for you to unpack after you rest."

"You didn't get much sleep last night either," she states in protest.

"Ahh, but I slept each night before, and you did not," I remind her. "Besides, my boys need their mommy to rest so they can be healthy and happy."

"You're going to use them as a weapon often now, aren't you?"

I nod and point her in the direction of the bedroom then swat her behind to spark her movement. The adorable look on her face is worth another swat. Her wide eyes, her high brows, and her pretty little mouth forming the shape of an "O" with confusion of my actions cause me to bite my lip to stifle my laughter. It's going to be fun, throwing her off tilt with my actions, my demonstrations of love. She's not ready for me to put it into words, but I have no problem dropping a few hints with my actions while I wait for her to catch up. Again, I point to the bedroom, not fighting my laughter as she huffs loudly, spins on her heel, and stomps the entire way.

While they sleep, I quietly attempt to organize stacks of boxes in the living room, kitchen, and dining room to assist when we begin unpacking this evening and tomorrow.

Finding one box labeled master bedroom, I carry it from the kitchen area toward the wall near the bedroom door. I pause mid step. Quirking my head to the side, I realize the humming noise I hear is coming from the box in my arms. When I spin it around, I find it's labeled "Master Bedroom, Ryan's Nightstand."

Curious, I turn, setting it on the kitchen island. Pulling the tape from the top, I lift one flap then the other. Inside, I find books, lotions, manicure essentials, fuzzy socks, and...

What have we here? I grab a toy. It's not on, so I grab the other. My mind fills with visions of Ryan as I turn the device this way and that, searching for the power switch. Finding the push button buried flush beneath the purple silicon covering, I finally succeed in silencing the device.

Part of me wants to comb through the rest of the box's contents to possibly uncover other hidden treasures, but I feel I've invaded Ryan's personal space enough for one day. Not finding any batteries to remove, I place the two toys carefully back in the box before setting it near her bedroom door. I lean against the wall, eyes closed, lip pulled between my teeth, enjoying visions of Ryan naked under her sheets, writhing in ecstasy, a toy in her hand.

After many long moments, I shake away my naughty fantasies. In her life filled with tragedies, I doubt she remembers she still owns the vibrators or found herself in need of the release they provide. I feel sleezy for thinking such thoughts with all she's dealing with.

I cross the living room busying myself arranging more boxes, hoping that Ryan soon finds herself happy in a life where orgasms are back on the table, orgasms delivered by me and by vibrators.

32

RYAN

An Hour Later

I slowly open the bedroom door, quietly slipping through, then leave it open a crack. I rub my eyes as I maneuver my way through the stacks of boxes and furniture cluttering our new living room. From here, I see the kitchen and dining room look much the same and are also void of people.

I listen from the top of the stairs, hearing nothing from the basement. I decide to look in the garage. Here they are. The five movers are sitting on the truck sides, bumper, and a dining room chair, still wrapped in plastic wrap. While they drink from their thermoses, Lewis leans against the truck, his shirt off and a beer in hand. *I thought he drank them all last night so he wouldn't have to move them. Hmm... Maybe he bought more while buying snacks this morning.*

I'm not sure which I find more appealing right now, Lewis's bare chest and sculpted abs or the ice-cold beer he holds near his navel. *Stupid pregnancy hormones.* I attempt to shake off the thoughts of the sexy man in front of me. I haven't been lifting or working in this heat, but a beer would taste good right now. After carrying and giving birth to twin boys, Lewis had better wait on me hand and foot, delivering me beer or wine anytime I feel like it.

"Hey, honey," Lewis greets as I walk down the driveway.

"Working hard?" I tease.

The movers all look in my direction, not sure how to take my comment.

"Hey, guys," I greet. "It's looking good in there."

The men relax, realizing I'm teasing. I stop in front of Lewis, and he pulls me into his side. The heady scent of his sweat causes my head to spin. I lean my cheek on his shoulder.

"I slept too long," I murmur.

"No such thing," he replies. "I knew you were tired."

"I can't believe Ian's still asleep," I say, looking into his eyes. "I should go back in; he'll be up soon."

Lewis kisses the tip of my nose, letting go of me. I step away quickly so I can avoid the chance he might swat my behind again. He's in a weird mood today; it must be all of the excitement from the move and sonogram.

I'm not allowed to carry boxes according to my new pregnancy tyrant, so I unpack the two boxes in the kitchen then wait for the next time I see Lewis to ask him to bring me two more from the dining room. I unbox a couple more for the kitchen before I move to unpack the bathrooms.

"The new bedroom furniture is all set up. Ready for more?" Lewis asks, placing a box on the island for me.

I come back with, "That's what she said?"

"Nice," he grins, extending his fist for a pound against mine. Instead of moving on, he quickly wraps his hand around my fist and tugs me closer. "I've ordered pizza from Truman's Tavern; it should be here soon." He brushes hair from my face. "After this box, you should take a break. Go play with Ian until the food arrives."

I roll my eyes, not even trying to hide it from him. With each passing day, the pregnancy becomes more real to him. I try to remember that and have patience with his overprotectiveness. Carter tried to shelter me early in Ian's pregnancy, and I had to sit him down and place limits on his demands. I should do the same with Lewis.

Halfway through the next box, I realize I need my stepladder to finish it. I find my stepstool in the dining room, unfold it, and place it near the counter beside the sink. With Carter's mom's serving dishes in hand, I climb the steps, reach above my head, and slide the bowls into the upper cabinets.

"Freeze," Lewis demands sternly.

I roll my eyes and blow out a loud breath, nearly jumping out of my skin when his hands grasp my hips from the floor behind me.

"What do you think you are doing?" he growls.

"I thought this was the best place for them," I explain. "Where do you think I should put them?"

"Why are you on a ladder?" His lower tone hints at his unhappiness with me.

"It's a stepstool with only three steps," I start to protest, defending myself.

"I should put things up there. You're pregnant and shouldn't be climbing," he states. "I'll help you down."

I open my mouth to argue but think better of it. He's nervous I'll overdo it with the twins, and I can't blame him. I descend the steps, his hands still on my hips, gripping tightly. Safely on the floor, he spins me, not removing his grasp. I look up at him through my lashes, reminding myself he's a first-time father.

I watch as his eyes transform from frustration into something else, gazing into mine. He lowers his forehead to mine for a quiet moment.

"I need you to let me take care of you," he murmurs. "I need to know you and the babies are safe."

I nod, though it's difficult with our heads touching.

33

LEWIS

Weeks Later

"This is bad, right?" I ask Ryan.

"We need to take him to the hospital now!" she demands, rocking his tiny little body in her arms. "Get the car."

Out of my element, I do as she requests. I'm in the driver's seat, navigation set for Blank Children's Hospital when she slides into the back seat, keeping Ian in her arms. I want to argue that he's safest in his car seat but think better of it.

I pull from the driveway, as carefully as I can, driving over the speed limit with my flashers on the entire way. I want to ask questions, but I feel the only way I can help now is to drive.

When we arrive, in a whirlwind, Ryan leaps from the back, disappearing inside. I find a parking spot then dart inside, unsure where to go to find them. I look in all directions for Ryan and read the directional signage but have no idea where to go.

"Are you Mr. Howard?" a man in scrubs asks. "Excuse me. Are you Mr. Howard?"

My mind finally registers his words. I nod.

"Right this way," he instructs, walking briskly, and I follow.

We scurry down a long hallway, through a set of fire doors, and around a corner. I breathe a sigh of relief when Ryan runs towards me. I scoop her into my arms, unable to hold back my tears any longer. I don't break our embrace, and I don't ask questions. I simply hold her, my heart racing a million miles per hour.

Ryan's palms move to my pecs, and she lifts her eyes to mine.

"I'm sorry," she sobs.

I shake my head. "Nothing to apologize for. Where's Ian? What do we do now?"

"They... They've... He's with the doctors..." she finally says.

I take her lead, wiping my tears and attempting to steady my rapid breathing. She attempts to take a step back, but I keep my hold on her; I need her to ground me.

"We should wait over here." Her hand in mine, she leads me to a waiting area.

I'm thankful no other families inhabit the chairs. I don't think I could interact at this point. Seated, I wrap my arm around her back, pulling her tightly to my side. If I can't hold Ian, I must hold her. Waiting in silence, I've never felt so useless.

I promised Carter I'd keep them safe. I thought we'd been careful in our endeavors to protect Ian from germs. I wash my hands more now than any other time in my life. I can't believe how fast his normal little coughs morphed into chronic coughing, vomiting, and a sky-high fever.

He's been sick for over a year. I've never forgotten that fact. Naively, I believed we were managing his leukemia. Now, I see the horrors she emailed me about for so many months. A chill moves through me at the thought of Ryan, a recent widow, dealing with this on her own. I push down my fear; I need to be strong for both of them.

"Carter, brother, if you can hear me, please guide Ian through this." I send my silent prayer toward heaven. I know my brother's doing everything he can to help his son. I need to have faith, faith enough for all of us.

―――――

No one should ever have to see a child hooked up to so many tubes. His body's so little. I curse the plastic barrier between us, even though I know it's vital for his protection. I'm thankful they even let us in the room with him. I've synced my breaths with his on the ventilator, willing it to keep him alive. When Ryan exits the bathroom, I prepare for my next battle. I'm torn between Ian and her, unsure how to help either of them.

Whatever It Takes

"I want you to go home and get some rest," I instruct, raising my palm to her when she readies an argument. "I'll stay with Ian, and I promise to call with any changes. You need a good night's rest—for you and the twins—and you won't get that here. Please. You know I'm right."

To my surprise, she doesn't put up a fight. She stands at Ian's bedside, her open hands pressed to the plastic sheet cocooning him. I see her lips move but hear not a word.

When she approaches, I hold her in a tight hug, kissing the top of her head. As she looks up to me, I'm sure this is the right decision. Her bloodshot eyes beneath her heavy lids and the yawn she doesn't try to disguise give her away.

"I've arranged for a car to drive you home." This is where she chooses to fight me. "I need you to be safe; you're too tired to drive. You can take a car back here tomorrow. Please give me this peace of mind."

She crosses her arms over her chest, shooting daggers in my direction. I'm not phased; she'll thank me for this tomorrow. I allow her to find her own way downstairs, settling into my chair for the long night ahead.

34

RYAN

Weeks Later

My eyes squint at the bright afternoon sun filtering in through my bedroom mini blinds. Slowly propping myself up on one forearm, I can't believe I fell asleep. My laptop sits on the bed beside me, open but asleep. Ian naps on the other side of it, surrounded by pillows to prevent him from rolling off the bed. I glance at my cell on the bedside table and find it's past four; I fell asleep for over an hour.

I close my computer, placing it on the table, then set a pillow in its place. Satisfied that Ian is safe, I tiptoe around the house, attempting to hear where Lewis might be. I follow sounds into the kitchen.

He's leaning against the counter, his thumbs flying over his phone screen.

"Hey," I interrupt.

"How was your nap?" he asks, tucking his phone into his back pocket as he walks towards me.

"I didn't mean to fall asleep," I state. "I wasted an hour I could have been working."

"There's still time," he says. "I'll entertain Ian if he wakes up. Follow me. I want to show you what I've been working on."

I follow him from the kitchen into the garage. He's placed a wooden table next to the door leading to the kitchen. On it I see wipes, hand sanitizer, and disinfectant spray among other things.

"What's this?"

He shifts his weight from one foot to the other before explaining, "It's a germ station. I put one by the front door, too." He smiles proudly. "I've read that it's important that we social distance and keep Ian from as many germs and viruses as possible. His treatments lower his immunity, so we need to ensure we don't infect him. When we get back from errands or have a guest, we'll disinfect head to toe and spray anything we plan to bring into the house."

It's sweet, maybe a bit overboard, but sweet that he's taken this upon himself to keep Ian safe.

"I purchased disinfectant wipes for each room of the house, too." He fiddles with boxes of face masks and rubber gloves, organizing them on the tabletop. "Can you think of anything else we should do?"

"Nope. I think you have everything covered. You've been a busy beaver," I tease.

"That's what she said," he jokes.

"Umm..." I bite my lips to prevent my smile. "That one didn't work. You'll need to try harder."

"That's what she said," he laughs.

35

LEWIS

The Next Week

After one night of rubbing Ryan's back to help ease her into sleep, it's now our new routine. I slide into Ryan's bed while she completes her bedtime rituals. I have no idea how she keeps track of which lotion and cream goes where; it seems like too much work, but her soft, flawless skin assures me it works.

I fold the covers back on her side of the bed when she turns off the bathroom light and enters her bedroom. She's still rubbing lotion into her elbows as she approaches. With a smile on her face, she pulls the covers over her waist then reaches to turn off the light on her nightstand. I watch as she fluffs her pillow in the faint light from the street, filtering through the blinds. Perfectly positioned, I turn on my side, extending my hand to rub her back.

I rub her each night, hoping to ease her quickly into sleep. With her constant worry of Ian and her growing babies' bump, she rarely sleeps more than four hours at a time. Everything I've read stresses the importance of rest during her pregnancy, so I do my best to give her four solid hours now, two hours near morning, and a nap or two with Ian during the day. Of course, she fights me tooth and nail; most of the time, she gives in when I remind her Ian needs her healthy and rested.

My fingers lightly massage then gently trail up and down, up and down. I love when her body relaxes under my touch. I enjoy my effect on her. It fuels me to continue stroking her back for over half an hour before I hear her breaths even out. I pause, my hand still touching her back to ensure she sleeps. Moments pass with no movement on her part, so, my task complete, I roll onto my back.

This is the part of the night where I contemplate everything. *Should I remain in her bed to ensure she sleeps well tonight, should I sleep on the sofa to listen for Ian and her, or should I head downstairs, to my room, far from the sounds they might make tonight? Should I make her breakfast in bed and confess my undying love for her in the morning or wait?* Lucky for me, sleep sweeps me away within minutes, rescuing me from hours of what ifs and plans playing like movies in my mind.

Ryan

My eyes open, finding the room dark and quiet. *Hmm... No lights or noises on Ian's monitor. I wonder what woke me?*

Umm, hello! I peer over my shoulder, finding Carter tucked to my back—well, spooning is more like it. Every inch of him presses into every inch of me. I marvel at his warmth, his touch, and his hardness pressed to the small of my back.

Oh. My. God! I dart across the bedroom and stand, hand to my mouth, my back against the wall. The air feels heavy in my lungs as my heart threatens to beat through the wall of my chest. I can't breathe.

That's not Carter. He's not my husband. That's Lewis, my brother-in-law, my best friend, and he has a massive boner while holding me.

I want to believe he's asleep, that he's dreaming of his mystery woman... Try as I might, my hand to my mouth doesn't hold in my wail.

36

LEWIS

Later

Ryan's wail jolts me from my dreams. I reach to her side of the bed—it's empty. I sit up, scanning the room, listening for any sign it might be something with Ian. I find her against the wall, trembling.

I scramble from beneath the sheet, closing the gap between us. I extend my hand but freeze mid-air when she flinches. *What has her this afraid?*

"Ry," I murmur, "what's wrong?" My eyes beg her to open up to me, to let me help.

She shakes her head, tears dripping from her chin with the movement.

"Honey, was it a dream?" I ask, needing to fix it.

She shakes her head. "I can't…" She flees into her bathroom, locking the door behind her.

"Ry, talk to me," I beg, my palm and cheek against the door. I hear her sobs. " Let me in," I softly order, silently praying she'll unlock the door and allow me to hold her. My need to hold her is bone deep.

She's mine. She's always been mine. She was my first love, my only love, and she will be my last. It's time I let her know it.

I hear the click of the lock, watch as the knob moves ever so slowly. I don't rush her. I allow her to open up to me at her own pace.

Whatever It Takes

She's looking up to me through her wet lashes, and my heart aches. *Tell me. Tell me what's wrong. Please.*

"When I woke up..." she whispers. Closing her eyes, she draws in a long breath through her nose before continuing. "It felt... I didn't know where I was."

In her chocolate eyes, I see her pain and her fear.

"You just need a while to get used to our new place," I remind her.

"That's not it," she states. "I overreacted. It was nothing."

I know better.

"I need a snack," she informs, squeezing past me on her way to the kitchen.

Confused, I follow her.

Middle of the night snacks in the kitchen together... We've dined like this hundreds of times. She keeps saying it's just like college. That's true, but this time, I plan to tell her how I feel. I won't waste another day.

I go through the motions of eating bites from Ryan's fruity cereal, not tasting it. While Ryan slurps from her spoon and crunches as she chews, I attempt to work up my nerve.

"Do you dream about her?" Ryan asks out of left field.

"Huh?"

"I'm wondering if you still dream about your mystery woman," she reiterates.

"Um..." I delay. *How should I answer this? Honestly or totally honestly? Perhaps this is my opening. Here I go.* "I love you," I blurt.

Ryan continues eating her cereal, unphased.

"Ry," I demand her attention, my index finger pulling her chin my way. "I love you."

"I know," she mumbles through her mouthful of cereal.

"Okay. Let's forget your cereal," I say, pushing her bowl and spoon across the counter from her. "I need to share a story with you."

"Can it be a bedtime story? I'm needing a few more hours before Ian wakes up in the morning," she states.

"I'd prefer to tell my story sitting up." I spin her stool so she faces me, our knees touching.

"This had better not be a ghost story. You know they give me nightmares." She smiles, only half teasing.

"Remember the weekend Carter came to college to visit me for the first time?" I begin, heart racing.

Ryan nods, preparing to speak, but I halt her with my palm. "Ah, ah, ah. I'm talking. You're listening," I tell her. "Zip it." I make gestures with my fingers, zipping my lips, as I hope she will and listen to me. "Lock it." Then I pretend to toss the key over my shoulder.

She giggles, locking her mouth shut.

"In my failure to act, Carter hatched a plan. He asked the girl I was interested in to go out. He planned to talk me up, but it turned into a date."

I watch her face as she works through the list of possible girls I knew back then. I bite my lips, witnessing the moment she gets it. *She's* the girl. *She's* the one. Now, she knows. Time for me to lose the humor and lay it all out for her; time to tell her everything.

Okay. Now what? My mouth dries, and the air grows heavy. I push down a large gulp, never pulling my eyes from hers.

"It's natural for you to have feelings for me while I carry the twins," she attempts to explain.

"True, but I've always loved you," I continue, rising from my stool and standing inches from her. "For me, it was love at first sight."

She shakes her head, unable to fathom my announcement.

"Here, sit down," I instruct, pointing at the nearby dining room chair.

I'm serious. That much is certain. My eyes remain on her, not fidgeting around the room, and my jaw is relaxed, not clenching. Her mouth opens; words don't come out, however.

"You caught my eye in our first Business Law class." I smile. "That's why I asked to join your study group; I wanted to spend more time with you."

Again, her mouth opens. This time, I place two fingers over her lips to quiet her. Her eyes cross when she looks at them, causing me to chuckle.

"Take a sip," I order, placing a water bottle into her hand and guiding it to her lips. "Slow. You don't look good."

I watch her lips wrap around the mouth of the bottle. I'm distracted; I need to refocus.

"We devised a plan for Carter to be my wingman to get you to go out with me," I murmur, back on my stool in front of her. "Carter fell for you. I couldn't blame him. I mean, who wouldn't fall for you?"

She presses the cold water bottle against her overheated cheek. She draws in a long breath, counting to five, then releases it with a five count.

"I couldn't stand in his way—in your way. You shocked the hell out of me when you accepted a date with him. If Carter made you happy, I told myself I had to let him."

My palms on her knees burn. My body's overheated, and my touch sears. She raises her gaze from my hands back to my face. There she sees it. I'm serious. I'm telling the truth.

"He did make you happy, and he was head-over-heels in love with you," I claim. "So, I stepped aside, happy for the two of you."

"Crrraaapppp! It's me! I'm the mystery woman," she cries. "I'm the reason you left the country, left your family…" She lets her realization hang between us.

"Carter tried to talk me out of it more than once," I state, my eyes searching her face. "Nothing else worked; I had to get away."

"Away from me," she states, venom in her voice. "I'm the reason you left. I'm the reason for everything. You missed the birth of your nephew because you couldn't be near me."

"No." My tone startles her. "I couldn't let you go. I couldn't get over you. That's why I went away. You did nothing. I was to blame."

37

RYAN

Back in My Room

I sit on the edge of my bed, shock preventing me from moving. *A fool—I'm such a fool. How could I not know Lewis had feelings for me way back then, and Carter planned to help his brother ask me out? I'm a blind idiot. This changes everything—every conversation, date, and touch. They betrayed me, they lied to me, and they kept this secret between them all of these years. I'm the fool, none the wiser to their truth.*

Carter knew... The air evaporates, the room spins, and my blood feels like lava in my veins. *Carter knew? My husband, his twin, knew he was into me?* My entire world tilts on its axis. I can't breathe, and I can't stand.

My mind and heart war between hurt and hope. I've much to mull over; I need to rethink everything. *My best friend turned brother-in-law loves me and has loved me for six years. I'm the reason he took the job overseas, I'm the reason he wasn't here when I gave birth to his nephew, and I'm the reason he missed the final months of his brother's—his twin's—life. I caused Lewis's pain; I caused his family pain. I made a mess of it all.*

I flop on my bed.

Why did he find me unapproachable? What made it hard for Lewis to ask me out?

Why didn't Carter feel he could share this secret with me? Did he not trust me? Did he think I led Lewis on or was to blame for his love through the years?

I stand, shaking out my arms, while flexing my fists open and closed. I roll my neck from the left to the right and back, attempting to release the stress tightening it.

Lewis... Where does this leave Lewis and me?
He loves me, claims it's more than friendship.
I love him. But do I love him more than friendship? What does that say about me? Does this betray my husband's memory? How do I face him now? And how can we remain friends?

I pull up the mini blinds, peering out my bedroom window, unseeing. We *are* more. Flashes of small touches—his pecks upon my cheek, my forehead, my crown, and his long hugs, his rubbing my back—flood my mind. I thought it was all friendly because I'm carrying his babies. I brushed much of it off as sympathy.

Why? Why me? Why is my life so complicated?
Why have so many hardships found me in the past two years?
Did I cross lines along the way, between Carter and Lewis? Did I bring this upon myself?
What should I do?
I need him; I can't lose him.

For many years, he was the only one I could go to. He gets me, all of me, everything about me. He understood me better than Carter ever did.

I need him; I'll always need him.
I shake my head.
How many lines have we already crossed?

I woke up thinking of him as my best friend and brother-in-law. Now, he's more.

Should I want more? Do I deserve more?
How do we proceed from his proclamation of love? Where do we go from here?

My head swims, my stomach aches, my muscles feel weak, my hands tremble, and my rapid breaths are the only sounds in the room.

Pull. It. Together. I arch up onto my toes with my hands at the small of my back. Too stressed to sit, I pace back and forth. I need to come up with an answer. We live together, so I can't avoid him forever. It's best if I deliver my thoughts to him while Ian sleeps, but I'm not sure what I should say. I climb onto my bed, laying on my back, and stare at the ceiling. I won't be able to sleep until I figure out what to do. *Heck, I may not be able to sleep after I talk to Lewis.*

"Carter," I whisper, "help me, please. Give me a clue what to do."

First one then the other baby kicks. "That's what the two of you were like, sharing a womb." I grin. It's a sign. Identical twins, alike just as their father and uncle were, no matter what.

38

RYAN

The Next Morning

I shoot upright in bed, my eyes scanning the entire bedroom. *Alone. I'm alone. Dream. It's a dream.* My heart pummels my chest as I struggle for breath.

Was it Carter or Lewis? Which one was it, and how could I not tell the difference?

I should know the difference. It felt real, his touch and kiss. Who was it?

I will my breath to even out. I know why I had this dream. Lewis's admission stirs up feelings. I love them both in their own ways. They're two very different people despite their looks.

I like having Lewis here. I can't imagine my future without him at my side. I'm carrying his sons, so we're tied together.

If I allow myself to explore... If I allow myself to love him, will my dreams, my subconscious, haunt me? Will I wake, covered in sweat, full of fear every night? Can I love Lewis without constantly comparing him to his brother? Can I open myself up to the possibility of a life with Lewis?

I want to. The pulse of excitement humming through my veins outweighs the fear. I'm going to try.

Perhaps if I try, he'll be there for me. Maybe with him by my side, I'll survive another punch. Maybe he'll help put me back together.

I'm tired of being alone, being strong.

I pace toward the window. *It's not fair to ask another to carry my burden.*

I walk back to the door. *He's already wearing the same pain as me. He lost Carter, too. He feels the weight of Ian's illness. If he didn't, I wouldn't consider this. His shoulders strain like mine.*

I walk halfway toward the window, stopping to pivot midway. *Together, we'll face it, perhaps even find a bit of comfort in each other.*

I nod to myself, hands upon my hips. I guess now I need to share my decision with Lewis.

Before I do, there's somewhere I need to visit.

An Hour Later

"Part of me is really pissed at you right now. I'm mad that you didn't tell me the whole truth of why Lewis ran. Another part of me is frustrated you aren't here to help me with Ian's leukemia," I tell Carter's headstone. "I miss you. I miss you every hour of every day. Ian reminds me so much of you." For several long minutes, I play with blades of grass, attempting to quell my tears in order to continue.

I look up to heaven. "I'm sure you know the real reason I'm here today." I watch three small, puffy, marshmallow clouds skate above on the pristine blue sky.

"How messed up is this? My mind's still reeling." I shake my head. "The two of you, brothers, identical twins, both have a thing for me. I know I'm a lucky girl, but I'm not sure where I go from here."

What will we be? We'd be a couple, yet brother and sister-in-law. He'd become Ian's father and still be his uncle. No matter how we look at it, we'd be a family.

That's all that matters. Family looks out for each other, family lifts each other up, and family stays together, no matter what. Family until the end. We're unorthodox, we don't follow social norms, yet we work. We're family in every way.

It shouldn't matter what others think. Few will know our unorthodox path to love, to children, and perhaps to marriage. My stomach flip-flops at the thought.

On the outside, we are the norm—two people in love, raising a family.

That's all they'll need to see, while on the inside, we'll know we're much more. We've survived many tragedies and made it through to happiness. We're best friends, we're strong, we're survivors, we're family, and maybe, we'll become more.

My insides tingle at the thought, the possibility of Lewis and me and what might have been if he'd told me how he felt, asked me out himself in college.

I shake it off. I wouldn't have Ian; I wouldn't know how very precious every moment is. I'm stronger because it happened, and I survived. Perhaps we're stronger and happier because he waited years to confess his feelings for me.

I place one palm on my heart and the other atop his headstone. "It's wrong. It's wrong for me to carry on a relationship with brothers. It's against bro-code and probably only encouraged in ho-code." I draw in a long breath.

"It'd be easy to move forward with him. My mind sees you, and I pretend he's you. But that's not me. He's my best friend, and I can't lose him. Without you at my side, I need him desperately."

"I swear I never, and I mean *never*, thought of him as anything more than my best friend and your brother." My heart hammers against my palm on my chest. "But after his declaration... I can't believe I'm considering this. I... He..." I release a frustrated growl.

"If you knew about his desire to ask me out in college, and you came to help him achieve that..." *Crap!* I wipe tears from my cheeks. "You approve right?" I close my eyes, lifting my face to heaven. I allow the gentle breeze to fill my nostrils and warm sun to bathe my face. "I wish you could give me a sign, something to let me know you're okay with Lewis and me." I pause, waiting for a sign that doesn't come.

In the driver's seat, I press the button to start the ignition, preparing to make my way to Ian and Lewis, hands on the steering wheel at ten and two. I freeze. *It can't be.* I can't believe my ears. It's "our song" on the radio.

Removing my hands from the steering wheel, I lean my head back, and I'm transported back years to an in-depth, late-night conversation with Carter. Although we discussed every word of the lyrics, as I listen now, it has a completely different meaning. I shake my head, realizing Carter didn't share how true to life this song really was all of those years ago.

A large smile slides upon my face at the sound of the Spin Doctors singing *Two Princes*. It's ironic now that I know the twin brothers both wanted me and vied for my affection. It holds more meaning as I see the two princes as the two twins—Carter and Lewis.

"Carter," I call, looking toward heaven, laughing, "I got your message. I love you. Please, please, please continue to let me know you're here with Ian and me from time to time."

I laugh through my tears. I asked for a sign; message received.

Back at the house, Lewis moves through the morning as he has for many weeks. We spend the afternoon reading books, and I take a nap with Ian. While Lewis fixes dinner, I play with blocks with Ian on the kitchen floor. Then, I offer to load the dishwasher, allowing the boys time to play before bed. With each passing minute, excitement grows within me. I need to share my decision. I'm about to explode.

"Ryan," he hollers.

"Yes?" I draw out, ready for our conversation.

"Can you please bring me a water?" he asks.

What? Is he serious? A water? "Can you bring me a water?" Not a *"Have you thought about our discussion?"* Not a *"Have you made a decision?"*

I snag a water from the door of the refrigerator and deliver it to Lewis on the living room floor as he plays cars with Ian.

Ian is the miniature version of his father and thus the miniature of Lewis. They're adorable, and I can't resist snapping a photo to capture this moment. Then, I stare at the image on my screen.

"Hey, Mommy," Lewis calls, interrupting my sappy moment. "You should come down and join us."

I nod, placing my phone on the coffee table, then crawl on all fours toward the boys. Ian smiles, pushing a car in my direction.

"Thank you," I smile. My boy's learning to share.

We spend the next half an hour pushing vehicles around the carpet. As time passes, Ian's head lays on his left arm, and he pushes his car slower and slower.

"Bedtime," Lewis tells Ian, gathering him into his arms. "Wave good night to Mommy."

I pause in picking up the blocks and cars to smile and wave to my guys. "Good night," I call after them.

With the toys in the basket, I straighten the sofa cushions then return to the kitchen to scrub the pan I left soaking.

"How about some grape juice?" Lewis asks upon joining me in the kitchen.

"Sure," I reply, bending over the sink. After rinsing the suds from the pan, I take the proffered juice in a wine glass with a smile.

"It's a nice night. Let's sit on the front porch," Lewis suggests.

I nod, following his lead. The porch is small, holding only a decorative planter on each side of the front door. Lewis takes a seat on the top step, and I do the same. We sip our drinks for several long moments, observing the neighborhood children riding their bikes in the cul de sac while parents sit in folding chairs in their driveways.

A glint of sadness settles into my belly. I long for Ian to grow old enough to ride his bicycle with neighborhood friends. Although Lewis has given us a bit of hope for Ian's health, I don't dare to dream it true. I must not jinx it.

39

RYAN

Later

Lewis nudges my shoulder, lifting his chin in the direction of a woman pushing a stroller. "That's Dawn," he says.

I take another look at the woman as she approaches our block. She wears navy capris, white tennis shoes, and a navy and white striped top. She carries about twenty extra pounds on her frame, and a giant smile lights her entire face. She waves big, noticing me looking her way.

"Hello, neighbors." She stops on the sidewalk in front of our house.

I quirk my head when she doesn't move closer. Then I remember Lewis told her about Ian's immunocompromised illness when he met her shortly after we moved in. She earns points in my book for remembering to keep her distance.

"Enjoying this perfect evening," she notes. "Is your little one already in bed?"

"Yes," I answer.

"Riley's teething and fussy." She explains the toddler in her stroller who is not sleeping. "I thought another walk might calm her. Lord knows I needed a walk, too," she cackles. "Maybe I'll have myself a glass," she motions to the wine glasses in our hands, "when I finally get her down for the night."

Whatever It Takes

I stand, passing my juice to him. "I'll be right back," I murmur to Lewis.

"Ours is grape juice," I inform, rubbing my babies' bump as I approach Dawn, standing five feet away from the front of the stroller. "Who's this pretty girl?"

"This is my niece, Riley," Dawn smiles proudly.

I take in the toddler chewing on her fingers, excessive drool dripping from her chin, and her heavy eyes. I judge her to be close to Ian's age. She's his height but carries a healthier weight than he does.

"I'm Ryan," I greet with a small smile.

"I'm Dawn. We met your husband, Lewis, a few weeks ago."

I can't tear my eyes from her beaming face. I can see the perky, contagious aura Lewis told me about when he first met her.

"I shared my number with him. Please don't hesitate to call if I can ever be of help. I can run errands, babysit, housesit…"

"Thank you," I interrupt, trying not to be rude. "We try to keep our distance. Um…" I fidget with my hands in front of me. "With Ian, we have to be careful."

"Yes. I understand." She smiles sincerely. "I could always shop and drop items on your porch," she offers sweetly.

"Thank you. I'll keep that in mind," I answer honestly. She may come in handy.

I motion to her niece. "I believe we've bored her to sleep."

We chuckle and wave goodbye. I return to a smiling Lewis, holding his empty wine glass.

"She's nice," I state before sipping from my glass.

"I told you," he says, bumping his shoulder to mine.

"She thought you were my husband…" I raise an eyebrow.

Lewis simply smirks.

40

RYAN

Later

Back inside, the house is silent except for Ian's light breathing over the monitor in Lewis's hand. Taking the juice glasses from him, I hurry to the kitchen, refilling them then placing the empty grape juice bottle in the recycling bin. I linger a moment, glasses in hand, looking out the sliding doors but not seeing the backyard. The day's winding down, and I need to answer Lewis's declaration. I need him to know where I stand—where we stand.

I startle as his warm palm connects with the small of my back.

"Sorry," he murmurs near my ear, raising goosebumps on my neck. I allow him to take both glasses and follow him into the living room. We say nothing as we sit near each other on the sofa, sipping our drinks.

"Ready?" he prompts.

"I have an answer," I blurt before I lose my nerve.

A slow smile creeps across his face. I dare say he looks confident. I guess he has reason to. He's known me longer than anyone. We're alike, thus the reason we've been best friends for years.

I nod. When he doesn't speak, I begin. "You shocked me," I confess. "In the six years we've known each other, this is only the second time you've shocked me."

He quirks his head to one side. "The other?

"When you took the job in Dubai."

It's not lost on me that both times were due to his feelings for me.

"I love you. I've always loved you," I state, grasping his hand in mine. "Finding out the real reason for Carter's visit that weekend in college came as a shock. It angers me. I expected to be shocked, not pissed." I stare at my thumb, drawing circles on the back of his hand. "I'm mad that the two of you had this secret. The two of you kept it from me all of these years." I chuckle hollowly. "I thought Carter told me everything. Now, I know our marriage contained lies. He lied to me often when I spoke of your mystery woman and her effects on you."

I shake my head, chancing a glance up to Lewis's eyes before continuing. "He wasn't perfect. I'm not perfect, and I never claim to be. It hurts to learn this after so many years. The two of us," my fingers point from Lewis to me, "shared a connection before I ever met your brother. Now knowing the full story and your true feelings…"

I place my hand over my mouth to cover a yawn. When Lewis shakes his head at me and opens his mouth to speak, I hold a finger up to halt him.

"I'm willing to explore the possibility of a relationship between us. I'd be an idiot not to." I lock my eyes on his. "It's uncommon for a woman to have a male best friend. Perhaps there's always been something more lying in wait." I bite my lips, waiting for his reaction.

"You're quiet. Please, tell me what you are thinking."

"I meant it when I vowed to Carter that I'd care for Ian and you. I know how I feel about you; it's more than friends. I need you to understand, regardless of where our relationship goes from here, that I will be by your side. You can't get rid of me. We're adults. We'll handle this like adults. Should we become more, and it doesn't work out, I'm not disappearing. We'll need to find a way to get back to our friendship for the kids' sake."

He places his palms on my cheeks. "I need us to agree on that."

I attempt to nod, but his hold prevents my movement.

He shakes his head. "Attempting to hide my feelings for you was the hardest thing I've ever done. I think about you *every single day*. No matter what I try, my feelings never wane."

"Did I…?"

He shakes his head. "You didn't encourage me," he states. "It's you being you. Everything about you does it for me. It's all me and not your fault."

His liquid blue eyes melt my heart.

"I feel like such a fool that the two of you knew about this for years," I share. "I thought we kept nothing from each other, but…"

"You can't hold that against him." He rubs his hands down his face. "Telling you would have stressed your marriage, your relationship with me, his twin, and potentially rid you of your best friend. I vowed never to act on my feelings or tell you. He vowed to keep my secret, too. Please don't be mad at him. He did it for me."

"So, where does this leave us?" My finger points back and forth between the two of us.

He shrugs. "I don't know where to begin," he says. "I'm sure you'd like to create a list to organize your thoughts, but I can't wait that long," he teases. Well, maybe only half teases.

Ready to move along, I confess, "I'm afraid, shocked, unsure where we stand, and equally unsure where we go from here. I can't..." I draw in a shuttering breath. "I can't afford to..."

"You won't lose me," he states emphatically. "I'm here. I'm not going anywhere. This is still our house, and I plan to help Ian and you." He pulls in a deep, audible breath. "I needed you to know I love you as more than my best friend and sister-in-law. I've always loved you and can't live another day without you understanding that."

His face blurs in my tear-filled eyes. Feeling my lower lip quiver, I draw it between my teeth.

He extends his hand to cup my cheek. "I vowed to Carter I'd take care of you. I only ask that you don't compare me to him," he sighs. "I took a backseat for many years, and now it's my turn to act."

"Act?" I squeak.

"I've already started," he claims. "I've been open around you. When the urge to hold you surfaced, I pulled you near."

I nod, visions of cuddles, hugs, and pecks to my brow and cheeks scrolling through my mind. He's definitely been more affectionate. Now, I know why.

"I'm not going to stop," he states matter of factly.

I pull my lips between my teeth, my emotions rising at the weight of his declaration.

He pulls my arm, entwining his hand in mine.

"I love you," he murmurs, voice cracking. "Ry, I've always loved you." Hand still wrapped with mine, he places a kiss on the back of it.

"I love you, too."

The corners of his mouth turn up, his eyes shining.

"I know you love me, but in a friend and relative kind of way." He quirks his mouth to one side. "I hope, after professing my love for you, that you'll open up to the possibility of more for us."

At his wink, I nearly giggle as my eyelids strain to hold back my tears.

"As my best friend, you know me better than anyone else, but I want you closer still. Let me love you and open yourself up to the possibility of loving me, not as a friend or relative, but as a lover," he pleads. "Can you do that for me?"

My fingertips press into my lips and tears spill over my lower lids and cheeks while I nod.

He releases a loud breath in relief. "We won't press it; we'll take it slow and see where it goes." He smirks, his eyes dancing mischievously. "Our lives are crazy, and I don't want to add too much too soon."

I nod. "I'm not sure..." My voice quivers.

"Uh-huh," he shakes his head, eyes imploring me to understand. "No pressure, no assumptions, and no comparisons." He bends to my eye level, peering deep within me. "I can't replace my brother, and I don't want to. The time the two of you shared will always be yours. I'm not Carter, and I want what we share to be ours alone, free of expectations and comparisons. Got me?" His eyebrows rise in anticipation.

"I can try," I whisper.

"That's all I ask." He smiles and wraps me in a tight hug. "Finally," he growls near my ear.

I chuckle, my arms wrapped around him. It's a hug we've shared hundreds of times before, however this is more. My stomach flutters with fear, with excitement, and with the possibilities.

"We'll start with a date," he smirks, causing a pleasant tingle in my belly.

A date. Is he serious? We've known each other since college, we live together, and I'm carrying his twins. He wants to date me?

"That being said, we must be creative as our dates must occur here with Ian," he chuckles. "I've several ideas, so I'll plan the first date for tomorrow."

Hmm... I guess I'm going on a date tomorrow with my best friend, my brother-in-law, and the father of my unborn children. This should be interesting. Another yawn escapes, eliciting a laugh from Lewis.

"Off to bed with you," he orders, relieving me of my empty wine glass.

I slowly walk into my room, change into my t-shirt, and wash my face. Emerging from the master bath, I pause as I find Lewis sitting in his usual position on the edge of my bed.

He places a kiss on the tip of my nose, winking again. "Let me rub your back," he offers. "Ian will be up before we know it. Besides, the twins need you to rest."

Without arguing, I slide into my usual position, on my side, awaiting his touch. It's more than a back rub; everything is more. I allow him the fantasy that he'll help me fall asleep. There's no way I'll sleep. I have too much on my mind and too much to process. While my mind runs a marathon, I allow my body, and hopefully my babies, to rest.

Lewis

"I love you," I proclaim, needing her to hear me, to believe me.

My hands hang in midair as she rolls to face me. I place them on her hips. Tears well in her eyes, yet they do not fall. My eyes remain on hers, willing her to say yes.

"Let's start this chapter," I offer.

Her pink tongue darts out over her bottom lip before her teeth bite it. She leans closer, moving one painful inch at a time toward me. Unable to wait, I close the distance between us, my lips finding hers for the first time.

I've fantasized of kissing her too many times to count. The reality of this kiss far exceeds the fantasies. I fight the fevered need rising in me, keeping my mouth soft to hers, my tongue lazy in its explorations. *I'm kissing her. I'm finally kissing Ryan.*

When she pulls back, her palms cling softly to my chest, and her heavy-lidded eyes gaze up through her dark lashes. Her chest rises and falls quickly with her rapid breathing. My hand slides from her hip up to cup her cheek.

Her face in my hands, my eyes turn from her mouth toward her eyes. I smile the smile of a man crazy in love. She's finally mine, now and forever.

"I love you," I whisper.

"You may have mentioned that," she teases.

My hands tickle her ribs.

Ryan slinks her hand down my abs.

41

RYAN

"Ryan, we can't," he whispers.

We can't? Is he serious? He's the one that declared his long-standing love for me. He's the one peppering pecks to my cheeks and forehead while resting his hands on my hips and shoulders. *We can't? Like hell we can't!*

"Lewis," I murmur, in hopes of continuing, "I need you."

I see fear in his eyes.

"What's wrong?" I ask, halting my hands.

"We have to think of the twins," he states, shaking his head. "We need to wait."

Nope. Uh-uh. Waiting is not an option. I take his face in both my hands.

"Honey, the twins are safe," I state firmly. "Our doctor finds no issues with this pregnancy, so sex is safe." I tip my forehead towards him, my eyes imploring him to believe me. "You won't hurt the babies if you don't hurt me."

He attempts to shake his head, which is still in my grasp. "We can't risk it," he whispers, pain in his voice. "Ian needs…"

"I love you, Lewis Howard. I'm in love with you. I love that you want to give Ian the best chance at remission, but you are not listening to me. Hear me," I order, deepening my tone. "Sex is safe during pregnancy. It even says so in the pregnancy book you're *supposed* to be reading."

He sighs deeply, and I notice the hint of tears forming in his eyes. I close the distance between us, covering his mouth with mine. My lips move slow and soft upon his at first. In each kiss, I will him to feel my love, my strength, and my need. All of my doubt washes away. *I want this man.*

Still sensing a bit of hesitation, I take the lead. My playfulness pays off. Lewis's eyes spark to life.

Lewis

I marvel at Ryan's tenaciousness. Despite my worries, she's seeking this connection, this intimacy, this release. The reality of her in this moment far outshines the fantasies that consumed me for years. My insides war between my fear for the safety of the twins and my desire for her.

After we lay unmoving, her chest upon my chest, our labored breathing the only noise in the room, totally spent while still connected. I fight sleep, blissfully happy, holding Ryan atop me.

Ryan is resting beside me now, and our breaths even out. I feel the bed bounce up and down as a strange, muffled sound comes from Ryan. *Is she laughing or crying?*

"This is so screwed up," she states, her voice hoarse.

No! She can't be crying; she can't be comparing me to Carter. Shit!

"Ry," I call to her. Unable to see her face in the dark bedroom, my thumbs feel the corner of her eyes and find no tears.

"I'm six months pregnant with your babies, and we just had sex for the first time. So. Screwed. Up," she laughs.

So, she's not crying. I love this woman. I'm such an idiot for not asking her out back in college.

Ryan

The Next Morning

. . .

My eyes flutter open to the muted sunlight through the closed vertical blinds. *I slept. I never sleep. Ian!*

I knife up, frantically scanning my bedroom. I'm alone. Through the baby monitor, I hear Lewis speaking to my son. My fear subsides, and my heart rate begins to wane.

The pillow beside mine still holds the imprint of Lewis's head, causing memories of last night to flood my brain. *Who would have thought falling in love with my best friend would be so... Wow. Just wow.*

I'm in love with Lewis, and he loves me. If I believed in fairy tales, he'd be the dashing prince, riding in on a white steed, rescuing me from evil, planting a magic kiss upon my lips, and we'd live happily ever after in his castle.

But I live in the real world. It's a world where happy endings come and go; happy is a momentary state. I've learned the hard way to cherish the small things, take nothing for granted, and roll with the punches.

I'm currently in a happy-ish time of my life. Happy because I'm in love with Lewis and carrying his twins. -Ish because of Ian's leukemia.

I don't need fairy tales. They're fun to read but must be boring to live in. I could do with several years of happiness, though. Perhaps I'm due.

I pull Lewis's pillow to my face, inhaling his scent. I giggle like a middle-school girl with a crush. I'm choosing to live in the moment. I'm going to enjoy our new relationship, holding on to the joy it brings until the next shoe drops.

42

LEWIS

A Week Later

"Let's get married," I blurt, rubbing her back from my side of the bed.

Ryan's hand flies to her mouth as she coughs. She rolls to face me.

I find surprise when my eyes lock on hers.

"I'd like to be married when the twins arrive," I admit. "The last month or two of the pregnancy will be hectic with Ian's treatments and the babies might arrive early. I think it's better to do it sooner, rather than later," I ramble.

She licks her lips then pulls them tight between her teeth.

Here we go. Will she protest or agree? I'm prepared for an argument.

"I'm not sure a wedding will look right..." she begins.

"We could go down to the courthouse. Nothing formal, let's keep it simple," I suggest. "I'll do all the leg work; you'll just need to show up."

I smile, my eyes imploring her to agree.

"Okay."

Okay? Okay?

"No argument?" I ask astonished.

Ryan shrugs, "If you've been in love with me since the day we met and plan to be with Ian, the boys, and me forever, then I see no reason to argue."

That was easy.

I nod, a large smile bursting onto my face. "I'll make the arrangements tomorrow."

"So…" she draws out, sliding one hand up my chest. "Since we are now engaged to be married," she grins, one of her palms slides down my abs as she speaks. "We should celebrate."

My eyes wide. Ryan's insatiable appetite keeps me on my toes. She's exhausted from work, caring for Ian, and growing two little men in her seventh-month, sexy-as-hell babies' bump. Yet, she can't keep her hands off me.

"Ry…" I draw out, my voice husky.

"C'mon," she urges.

"The twins need rest," I protest.

She chuckles. "We'll be quick."

My brow furrows with my conflict.

"I'll sleep better if you help me," she urges.

I shake my head, releasing a long breath.

"Ry…" I groan.

———

Lewis

Later That Night

I tilt my head to the side, slightly above my pillow, trying to decipher the sound that woke me. It's faint, possibly from the kitchen. I quietly slip from under the sheets in an attempt not to wake Ryan. It's rare that she sleeps through the night, so I try to allow it when I can.

In the open space outside the bedroom door, I find the scratching sound comes from the front door. Slowly, I walk in that direction, not sure what might be making the sound.

With my hand on the doorknob, I pause, preparing myself for what I might find when I pull it open. Judging by the light sound, I assume I won't find danger. I turn the knob, readying myself for anything.

Standing on my doorstep, on our small front porch, is a long-haired, brown and black dog—a Weiner dog. It waltzes through the open door, brushing by my leg. I turn, the doorknob still in hand.

What. The. Hell?

Closing the door behind me, I stand awestruck as the little brown dog makes its way into the kitchen as if it owns the house. I follow in its steps silently.

I find it standing to the left side of the door to the garage, looking from the empty floor to me and back expectantly. Assuming this lost dog to be hungry or thirsty, I fill a small bowl with water, placing it near where he stands. When it immediately begins lapping at the water, I pat myself on the back for solving one mystery.

Done drinking, it walks the perimeter of the open living room, dining room, and kitchen, sniffing the floor and our furniture as if it knows this house and recognizes there are new furnishings. I follow behind, wishing I spoke dog to better understand this situation. After his investigation, the dog sits on the kitchen floor and looks up at me, tilting his head to the right then the left.

Hmm...

"Come here, little guy," I call, squatting down, summoning the dog towards me.

I reach out, stroking between his floppy ears, eliciting a whimper from him. Slowly, the dog inches closer to me, allowing me to rub his back. Growing more comfortable with me, it rolls onto its back, granting me access to rub his belly and allowing me to see he is, in fact, a male.

I shrug. *Good guess.*

He must be hungry. I open the refrigerator, scanning for any leftovers appropriate to feed a dog. Taco meat, salad, macaroni...hmm. Hotdogs! Ooh...Is that in bad taste? A Weiner dog eating weiner dogs... Again, I shrug. Hotdog it is. I pull out one, tearing it into bite-sized pieces on a paper plate and lowering it next to the water bowl. Pleased when he eats, I contemplate my next move. He belongs to someone. He has to have an owner missing him.

While he licks the plate, I bend down to his side. "Wanna spend the night?" I ask as if he might answer.

He sits, looking up at me.

"Let's go to bed," I offer, picking him up and carrying him to our room.

I know this is a bad idea. Ryan and Ian will instantly fall in love with this long-haired mop. They've lost enough. When his owner claims him, it will sting. I can't turn him back out into the night. He seems at home here, so I'll care for him until we find his owners. I pray it's tomorrow for his sake, for Ian and Ryan's sake, and for my sake.

The Next Morning

My feet slap heavily against the pavement as I slow my pace. Hands at my sides, I bend, gasping for each breath.

"Early morning run?" Dawn's voice greets from the sidewalk opposite me, hands gripping the stroller.

I nod, standing upright, hands still upon my sides. My five miles today, rather than my usual three, take their toll on my recovery time. I shuffle my feet side to side, my running shoes moving stray rocks as I do.

"Oscar!" Her voice raises in surprise.

I scan the neighborhood in search of the man she's talking to. When she bends down, patting her knee, I realize she's calling the Dachshund that appeared on our doorstep last night.

"Is he yours?" I ask.

She shakes her head. "The woman you bought the house from was his owner," Dawn states.

"Do you know how we might reach her?"

"She's in a skilled-nursing facility," she explains. "I assume her son kept Oscar."

"Any chance you know how I can contact her son?"

Again, she shakes her head. *Crap.* This means he'll be with us another day. That's one more day for Ian and Ryan to grow attached. That's one more day that makes it harder for them to see him go.

"So..." Ryan draws out while setting the table for dinner. "What did you uncover today?"

I hold in the breath I want to blow out slowly. I won't add my worry to hers.

I remove oven mitts from my hands, folding my arms across my chest, resting my hips against the stove. Then I shake my head.

"Really?" she asks, her voice rising excitedly.

I sense her growing excitement. This is exactly what I feared. The longer Oscar remains with us, the more attached we grow.

"Oscar's vet attempted to trace his new owner's information via his microchip," I explain, shaking my head. "It still shows Oscar living at this address, and no one knows how to find her son…"

She bounces up and down, her hands clapping in front of her chest. *She's actually clapping. I knew this would happen.* I don't fight my smirk, my eyes roving her beautiful face. This woman should always be smiling. It's truly a blessing to behold.

"Can we keep him?" Her voice sounds like a little girl's, full of hope.

I cannot deny her anything. Heaven help me if she ever learns this. I'm putty in her hand, and she owns me.

"Oscar's home is here unless his family comes for him," I state, proud to place the smile upon her face. "I guess I need to make a run to the pet store. Oscar needs a bed of his own and food dishes."

She giggles, wrapping her slender arms around my neck and melding her mouth to mine.

Ryan

Days Later

Lewis makes the gesture of brushing his hands off when he returns from Ian's room. I smile at him pretending it's an easy feat to get our little guy to fall asleep. On nights like tonight when he doesn't feel well, it's harder than normal. Case in point, it took him over 30 minutes tonight.

"Ready for me to put you to bed now?" he inquires, head tilted to one side.

Always concerned about the amount of rest I get each day, his worry gets annoying at times like now. I might be a bit tired, but there's something I need to take care of first.

"Come here." My words match my gesturing finger.

I grasp his hand, pulling him to sit on the sofa beside me. Before he can settle in, I lift my leg, shifting to straddle his lap.

"I guess that's a no for putting you to bed," he says, his voice a low growl.

"Not in the mood?" I challenge, one eyebrow raised.

Lewis

She's mine. This magnificent woman, amazing in so many ways, loves me, and I love her. Knowing she loves me proves the most potent aphrodisiac.

I shake my head at her, walking backwards, guiding her to our bedroom, unable to put away my giant grin. "I need a shower, and you need to get ready for bed. I'll be quick and rub your back."

"Nope," she states matter-of-factly. "I'm showering with you." Her eyes light up as her libido sparks back to life.

She may be the death of me. I constantly war with the safety of the pregnancy and keeping my woman happy. If she weren't pregnant with twins, if Ian wasn't desperately in need of a transplant, I'd allow Ryan to use my body all day every day.

In a flash, she's in front of me. She enters the bathroom, turning on the shower.

"Make it quick," I say, extending my hand for her to enter the shower before me.

"I don't like quick." She fake pouts, facing me under the stream of water.

I grab both forearms as they move towards me. "You can't overdo it. You need your rest."

She pouts. "Stop being the fun police and let me enjoy you."

I'm a weak man; I give in to her.

Minutes later, she is stepping from the shower.

"Off to bed with you," I order, swatting her booty playfully.

This time, she doesn't argue. She puts up no fight, simply waving over her shoulder at me before sliding into her robe.

I remain in the shower, lathering my body while basking in the bliss that is my life. When Ryan confessed that pregnancy hormones make her horny all the time, I didn't believe her. Four months later, I'm the luckiest man alive, reaping the benefits of her ever-thirsty libido. I traveled halfway around the world in search of a moment of escape after failing to find another, a proxy—it was always her. This woman, everything about her, does it for me—sweet, sweet euphoria.

In bed, I prepare to make my suggestion and argue until she gives in. I take in a deep breath, let it out, then it's go time.

"I think we should hire a nanny that's also a nurse to help us," I state, anxiously waiting for her arguments.

Head tilted, eyes assessing, Ryan remains quiet for the moment.

"Closer to your due date," I explain. "We'll have our hands full when the twins arrive. I'll be with Ian as he prepares for the cord blood donation, and then everyone has to recuperate afterwards." I pause, and she's still silent.

"I'll be at the hospital with Ian often, so I won't be here to help you with the boys. And when Ian is home, he'll be sick because of his chemo," I continue. "We will need help, and unfortunately, neither of us have family to help out."

Ryan purses her lips, eyes moving around the room as she contemplates.

Unable to take her silence, I prod her. "What do you think?" I ask.

"Um..." she draws out. "I don't like—" She holds out her palm, and I stop my interruption.

"I don't like the idea, but we *will* need help," she states. "I've been trying to come up with a plan. The only solution I thought of was holding off on Ian's transplant until after six weeks postpartum. I don't like that; I don't want to make him wait. Too many things can go wrong. He'll be quarantined before and after the procedure, and the twins and I will be somewhat the same for at least 6 weeks." She shrugs.

"I'd like to hire this person four weeks before your due date," I share, wanting to further explain my thoughts. "Twins usually arrive early, and you may need go on bed rest as it draws nearer. We can get to know the person before the twins arrive, and they can help as Ian starts donor protocol treatments. They can learn the house and help us set up routines. A nanny with nurse training would be perfect."

Ryan nods, smiling.

"So...?" I draw out. "Can I do some research?"

She nods. "I'd like to interview the person with you."

"Of course," I smile. "I must admit, I thought I'd have to convince you."

"I'm starting to realize I can't do everything on my own." She shrugs. "Life is simpler with help."

I smirk, knowing I'm the main reason she's learned that lesson.

43

LEWIS

The Next Week

"So, what do you think?" I ask Ryan, pulling my casserole from the oven.

Ryan sets plates and utensils at our places and Ian's cup on his tray then returns to my side as I find a utensil to serve the cheesy layers of my quesadilla casserole. It's a new recipe I hope Ryan loves.

"I like all three applicants," she states, moving a trivet to the center of the table tucked in our breakfast nook.

I follow her, hot pads on both hands as I carry the glass dish.

"I liked Danielle most," I share.

She nods.

"Who did you like?" I prompt.

I lift Ian into his highchair while Ryan places a plastic plate with sliced chicken and green beans in front of him before taking her seat next to mine. I serve her a slice of casserole then get mine.

"It's hard," she confesses. "I worry we will never know enough about any of the applicants to trust them with Ian or the twins."

"Ry, we've been over this," I soothe, attempting to calm her fears. "Nursing certification ensures they are trained medically to assist with Ian's medications, treatments, and any future complications."

She nods. "It's how they'll interact with Ian and the twins that causes me concern," she shares. "Without seeing them in action, it's a leap of faith that they are good with kids."

"Honey, we vetted their recommendations," I remind her. "Their previous employers gave glowing reviews of their interactions with their families."

"It's hard," Ryan reiterates.

"No one will be as good as we are with our kids, but we need the help." I play with my fork and a bite of food on my plate.

"If I have to choose one, I think it should be..." Ryan also pushes food around on her plate. "...Danielle."

Relief floods me as we agree on our future nanny and nurse. I worried we'd each want someone different and need to persuade each other through hours of discussion to choose one.

"I like how open she was in sharing about her own family and her reasons for choosing the field of nursing and to work with children." I pause, taking my first small bite, chewing quickly to continue. "You saw the way she looked at Ian. You can't fake that. She loves children; she'll be great."

Ryan swallows a bite, washing it down with water. "This is delicious," she croons, preparing to take another bite.

Before she does, I seek a final decision, placing my hand on wrist, pausing her fork midair. "So, we agree to offer the job to Danielle?"

"Yes," she chuckles. "Now, can I please eat?"

I remove my hand, allowing her to enjoy my casserole. It's a huge weight off my shoulders, knowing we'll soon have professional help with the kids. While I'm happy we have the means to secure help, I long for the day when Ian's healthy, and we can raise our three boys by ourselves.

44

RYAN

Later

At times, it felt as if those nine months would never end, but here we are. This morning, my obstetrician will induce my labor. By nightfall, I'll be the mother of three boys, and Ian will receive his cord blood cell donation. With the stress of Lewis spending the last two weeks at the hospital with Ian in preparation for the transplant, I'm surprised I didn't deliver the twins already.

I turn my phone's camera to display my IV bag to my right.

"They've started the oxytocin," I tell Lewis as I turn the lens back to me during our video call.

"Pain started yet?" he asks.

I shake my head. "I don't plan to be on the phone for that part of the delivery," I remind him.

"Hey, turn back to your IV again," Lewis urges.

I do as I'm instructed, wondering what he's up to.

"Ian, look what Mommy has," Lewis singsongs to my little guy.

Now, I know why he wanted me to show my IV.

"She has an IV just like you," Lewis says.

"Hi, honey," I call, moving the camera back to me.

Ian's heavy-lidded eyes and lack of movements from his sedatives and other medications are the reason he doesn't smile, wave, or speak to me. But I continue, needing him to hear my voice.

"Mommy loves you. Be a good boy for the nurses and doctors." I hate the sound of my voice. In it, I hear the weight of his hospital stay, today's procedure, and my fear for his health, both current and future.

Nurses flutter about my room, checking monitors and taking my vitals.

"Lewis, I think I need to let you go," I grit out through my contraction.

"Oh! Wow!" Lewis's eyes are wide, and his eyebrows are high. "Are you in pain?"

"Mm-hmm," I moan.

I don't open my mouth for fear my words might hurt him. In my discomfort, I don't want to take it out on him. He needs to be there for Ian and not worry about the twins and me. My contractions with Ian were not like this. These are stronger, closer together, and more intense; it must be the medications they use to induce my labor.

"I love you," I say quickly between contractions. "Give Ian a kiss for me." I hang up before Lewis responds, passing my phone to Danielle.

Lewis

My hand against the plastic surrounding Ian's hospital bed, tears fill my eyes. I'm alone on an island, desperate for contact, needing to be in two places at once.

I'm failing in my attempt to be a rock for Ian as he heads for his transplant soon. My thoughts focus on Ryan. Last time Danielle texted, they were wheeling her into surgery for a C-section. She assured me the twins were fine. Ryan's labor just wasn't progressing as the doctor would like.

My wife, my twins are a block away, but it feels like miles. She needs me, and they need me. I should be there to greet them when they enter the world and witness their first breaths. Although Ryan's a strong woman, her husband should be with her as she gives birth. I feel I'm letting her down. Ian needs me, though, and I know Ryan needs me to be here with him.

I'm torn. I'm torn between everyone I love. I feel helpless. There's nothing I can do for Ian here. I can't touch him or hold him. I can't take away his pain or cure him. I'm not with Ryan. I'm not holding her hand, wiping sweat from her brow, coaching her to breathe, or sharing in the joy of meeting our boys for the first time. I'm letting everyone down today.

My vibrating phone pulls me from my pity party.

Danielle: Boys here & healthy & Ryan's doing good
Danielle: Twin A 7lbs 2 oz
Danielle: Twin B 6lbs 13 oz

I breathe a sigh of relief, close my eyes, look to heaven, and thank God for watching over all three of them.

Me: Thank you
Me: Hug & kiss the boys for me
Me: Tell Ryan I love her &
Me: To call me when settled in room

My hand covers my smile, and I shake my head. *They're safe*. My boys are here, Ryan's good, and I can breathe a sigh of relief where they are concerned. Now, I need to focus on Ian and his procedure.

Lewis

Later

"I'm not sure what to say," I whisper into the empty room. Sadly, the last time I stepped foot in a church was Carter and Ryan's wedding. Thinking about it now, I started skipping church on Sundays in college, only attending when I visited my parents on weekends at home. I pray often; I pray, and I pray, and I pray. Today, it's not prayer; it's comfort I seek.

I take a seat in the second pew from the front of the hospital's tiny chapel. The dim gold lighting on the large wooden cross hanging at its center sets the tone. I'm here to wash away my oppressive fear and allow my faith to comfort me.

I'm utterly helpless. Ryan and the twins are less than a block away at Methodist Medical Center. However, with my social distancing to be near Ian, they might as well be in another state. I've video-called Ryan multiple times, and thanks to Danielle, I know the three of them are resting now. I need to be here for Ian. The Blank Children's Hospital staff accommodate our every need, but only God knows how Ian will fare with his bone marrow transplant.

Thus, here I sit, lifting everything up to God. My faith wanes a bit as I wait for Ian to return from his procedure. I couldn't spend another minute in his empty hospital room, and since I was constantly talking to God, I figured I might as well surround myself with the calming symbols of my faith.

I attempt to rid my thoughts of all the negative outcomes possible. I must have faith, faith that God takes Ian into his care, faith that Carter acts as Ian's guardian angel, faith that Ryan and the twins understand my absence, and faith that our love will see us through. The only thing I can do is lift everything up to heaven in prayer for several quiet moments.

"Lewis," the timid nurse's voice slices through the silence of the chapel, "Ian's on his way to his room."

Unshed tears burn my sinuses and flood my eyes. I turn and thank the blurry nurse peeking through the doorway. At the sound of the door closing, I fall to my knees in the aisle, facing the makeshift altar.

"Please…" I beg into my hands, folded in prayer in front of my face. "Please be with Ian. Lord, please be near him every step…"

I pause, noting the golden light around the large wooden cross twinkles in my teary vision. I hope it's a sign, a sign that Ian's never alone. I hope the transplant brings success and health for Ian. I hope…

Ryan

At The Same Time

. . .

I press the nurses' call button while fighting a yawn. When the OB nurse pops her head into my room, I motion for her to come in.

"The boys have full tummies," I inform her. "Can you take them back to the nursery?"

She nods.

"I think I'll take a little walk before I nap," I explain.

Her face scrunches. "Your doctor doesn't want you walking with your IV in." She smiles. "Only to the bathroom and back." She points to the closed door and back as she speaks.

I bite my lip, and tears well in my tired eyes.

"Honey," she draws closer, patting my forearm, "you should rest. You've got to be exhausted, having just given birth to twins."

I fan my face then shake my head.

"What is it?" she asks, concern upon her face.

"It's Ian..." My sob prevents me from continuing.

She looks at her watch. "It's today, isn't it? Umm... Okay. I'll roll the twins to the nursery. Then I'll come sit with you."

"I wanted...I want..." I release a frustrated groan at my inability to speak. Summoning all my strength, I pull in a long breath and release it. "I hoped to visit the chapel," I explain.

"Give me a minute," the nurse states as she walks out the door.

This will be the longest day of my life.

―――

I'm struggling to keep my eyes open in my quiet hospital room while the twins sleep soundly in their bassinets to the left of my bed and Danielle walks to the cafeteria for a meal. Thankfully, the nurse returns with a quiet rap on my door. Using my hands planted on the mattress on either side of my hips, through the pain, I push myself higher on the bed.

"I've brought reinforcements," she announces as two other nurses follow her to my bedside, Danielle trailing them. The final woman to enter my room is dressed in scrubs and wears a cap, facial mask, and covers over her shoes. She walks to the right side of my bed, lowering her mask only for a second. Her warm eyes and smile seem familiar.

Mask back in place she asks, "Remember me?"

At her words, my exhausted brain clicks; she's a nurse from the children's cancer ward, and she's been there during several of Ian's hospital stays.

"Since you can't be with Ian, I thought I'd come over for a quick visit." She pats my forearm. "Everything is going as planned for him. If you'd like, we can say a prayer."

I close my eyes and nod. These amazing women take time from their busy workday to help calm my nerves and fears for my son.

We join hands, and I keep my eyes closed as each nurse says a little prayer for my family. Tears escape the corners of my eyes; I don't fight them. At my turn, I opt for moments of silence. I allow my eyes to meet each of theirs, going slowly around the circle. It's my silent thank you for giving me this, for holding me up during this difficult time. I nod my head and wipe my tears. Understanding me, they quietly exit my room, Danielle closing the door behind them.

EPILOGUE

Two Years Later

Flames dance and crackle in our fire pit as we surround it with several couples from our neighborhood. My feet perch on the stone encasing it as my eyes watch the children through the nearby patio doors. With no movement in the portable cribs, I assume the twins are asleep while the older children, scattered on the floor on pillows, enjoy a Disney movie with popcorn. Feeling my eyes upon him, Ian turns away from the movie and waves at me, a big smile upon his face, then returns to the show. *Who knew how perfect Lewis's choice of home would fit into our future lives?*

"He asked me if he could stay up all night," Lewis murmurs, his lips near my ear, raising goosebumps on my neck. "I told him he could stay up until his friends leave."

"He'll never make it that late," I chuckle. "What a difference two years make."

We clink the neck of his beer bottle with the rim of my blue tumbler and take a drink. I enjoy spending time with our neighbors, turned friends, at our backyard BBQs, playdates, and celebrations. I enjoy the simple things in my daily routine like laundry for a family of five and tripping over the boys' toys.

"Our story belongs on Jerry Springer..." the couple from two doors down professes. "I set him up with my best friend in junior high, and they dated well into college. I was always the third wheel." She laughs. "Until my former best friend cheated on him, and we fell into bed together a couple of weeks later."

My eyes fly to Lewis; we share a knowing look. Our story isn't the normal boy-meets-girl fairytale story. Many would think us scandalous or question our ethics. We know we love each other and our boys. We are happy and healthy.

I think I'll tell him tonight...

"Hey, guys," I raise my voice to get everyone's attention. "I'd like to make a toast. Anyone need a refill?"

They check their current drinks and look to me to continue.

"Thank you for coming tonight. Our family cherishes our time with each of you and your kids."

Our friends lift their drinks, believing my toast to be over.

"Now for my announcement," I quickly interrupt before they all sip their drinks. "I need to confess, I'm not enjoying Dawn's famous margaritas." I lift my tumbler. "In fact, I won't be drinking alcohol for many months to come."

My female friends squeal, hop from their seats, clap, and hug me while the guys look on, confused.

"She's pregnant, dummies," Dawn announces to the lost guys.

"Seriously?" Lewis asks, rising, his wide smile reaching up to his sparkling blue eyes.

At my nod, he wraps me tightly in his arms. "I know we said we weren't planning on more children, but I love that God had other plans for us." He places his palm flat upon my stomach.

"Think we can handle four kids?" I ask, my voice breathy. "Heaven help me if it's a fourth boy." I giggle.

"Maybe it will be twin girls," he murmurs.

I stiffen. *Twins?* Four kids under four is one thing—five under four is another.

Lewis laughs at my fear. "We've got this," he vows, placing a kiss at the corner of my mouth.

My hands fly from his hips into his hair, holding him to me. I open my mouth, inviting him in.

"Uh-hmm," a male throat clears nearby. "She's already knocked up. Lewis, control yourself. There are children nearby," he teases, prompting our friends to laugh.

"To good friends, good times, and growing families," Dawn toasts.

Whatever It Takes

I don't wake everyday like the beauties with bouncy, shiny hair in the shampoo commercials. In our house, we don't break into song and dance while doing our chores as they do in musicals. Unlike the movies, my car doesn't always start, the lawn isn't always green, and our house is cluttered rather than pristine. Our life is far from perfect, and I absolutely love it.

Our road is rarely straight, and we maneuver several curves, abrupt forks, one-way streets, and slow-moving traffic flowing in only one direction. It's been a long hard journey to arrive at our happy place. At times, we hitchhiked, carpooled, called for a ride share, stood in the rain at the bus stop, braved the desert, relaxed on the beach, traversed forests, and lost ourselves in fields.

We've learned to revel in every sunrise and lazily enjoy warm sunsets. We do whatever it takes to survive the day and week. We fight, we kick, we scream, we climb, and we claw our way out. We're strong enough to wait out the storms to enjoy the sunny skies in our future.

With Lewis by my side, I embrace each moment, enjoy the sun, notice the smell of dinner cooking, and lose myself in the chaos of our typical mornings. To many, these are not special moments—to us, they're everything. Every minute of life is precious, both the big and small events. We live in the present, and we live life to its fullest.

Our lives resemble the infinity symbols I'm prone to doodle. After meeting in our college class, Lewis's and my life followed the figure-eight path, constantly intersecting. Some call it fate or Karma. I like to think of us as meant to be—inevitable—on our infinity path.

The End

TRIVIA:

1. The first and last names of *ALL* characters in this book are the names of famous authors. (Except the neighbor Dawn)
2. The character Dawn is based on my best friend. During a car ride, I explained my next series of books and she suggested I have one random character that appears in each book. Thus, I named the character after her and awarded her Dawn's positive spirit. In 2015 she was diagnosed with stage IV colon cancer. They found it late and it had spread throughout her body. She has chemotherapy every two weeks for the rest of her life. With all of this she's still a ray of sunshine and lifts others, like me, up. Her strength and selflessness inspire me to try and improve myself. She's the most upbeat and positive woman I know. I absolutely love her laugh.
3. What are the cardinal sins? The 7 deadly sins, also called 7 cardinal sins, are transgressions that are fatal to spiritual progress within Christian teachings. They include envy, gluttony, greed, anger or wrath, sloth, and pride. They are the converse of the 7 heavenly virtues.

ARE YOU SOCIAL?

Keep up on the latest news and new releases from Brooklyn Bailey

Please consider leaving a quick review on Amazon, Goodreads, & Bookbub.

ABOUT THE AUTHOR

Brooklyn Bailey's writing is another bucket-list item coming to fruition, just like meeting Stephen Tyler, Ozzie Smith, and skydiving. As she continues to write sweet romance and young adult books, she also writes steamy contemporary romance books under the name Haley Rhoades, as well as children's books under the name Gretchen Stephens. She plans to complete her remaining bucket-list items, including ghost-hunting, storm-chasing, and bungee jumping. She is a Netflix-binging, Converse-wearing, avidly-reading, traveling geek.

A team player, Brooklyn thrived as her spouse's career moved the family of four, fifteen times to four states. One move occurred eleven days after a C-section. Now with two adult sons, Brooklyn copes with her newly emptied nest by writing and spoiling Nala, her Pomsky. A fly on the wall might laugh as she talks aloud to her fur-baby all day long.

Brooklyn's under five-foot, fun-size stature houses a full-size attitude. Her uber-competitiveness in all things entertains, frustrates, and challenges family and friends. Not one to shy away from a dare, she faces the consequences of a lost bet no matter the humiliation. Her fierce loyalty extends from family, to friends, to sports teams.

Brooklyn's guilty pleasures are Lifetime and Hallmark movies. Her other loves include all things peanut butter, *Star Wars*, mathematics, and travel. Past day jobs vary tremendously from a radio station DJ, to an elementary special-education para-professional, to a YMCA sports director, to a retail store accounting department, and finally a high school mathematics teacher.

Brooklyn resides with her husband and fur-baby in the Des Moines area. This Missouri-born girl enjoys the diversity the Midwest offers.

Reach out on Facebook, Twitter, Instagram, or her website…she would love to connect with her readers.

- amazon.com/~/e/B0B57RYXZ2
- goodreads.com/BrooklynBailey
- bookbub.com/authors/brooklyn-bailey
- instagram.com/brooklynbaileyauthor
- facebook.com/BrooklynBaileyAuthor
- twitter.com/brooklynb_books
- pinterest.com/haleyrhoadesaut
- tiktok.com/haleyrhoadesauthor

ALSO BY BROOKLYN BAILEY

Ali's Fight

Cardinal Sins: Series of Stand Alone
Bend Don't Break
Behind a Locked Door
Chance Encounter
Starting Over
Whatever It Takes

Country Roads Series
Memory Lane
Dusty Trail to Nowhere
Fork in The Road
Take Me Home

Made in the USA
Middletown, DE
01 February 2025

70701754R00095